MUSIC CITY
CONFIDENTIAL

by Dan Tyler

EGGMAN PUBLISHING

A Miro Book

© 1996, Dan Tyler

Edited by Dagny Stuart and Adele Brown Tyler

Jacket design by Bill Tyler

Design/typography/production by TypeByte Graphix

"The Cowboy Blues" ©1996, Hamstein Stroudavarious Music
and Crossunder Music (ASCAP).
Words and music by Dan Tyler.
All rights reserved. Used by permission.

Library of Congress Catalog Card Number: 96–85873

ISBN: 1–886371–36–9

Eggman Publishing
3012 Hedrick Street
Nashville, Tennessee 37203
1–800–396–4626

Miro Books
P.O. Box 121227
Nashville, Tennessee 37212
615–297–3637

FOR, TO and WITH
ADELE

NASHVILLE, TENNESSEE
1992

ONE

The elderly black woman checked the wall clock hanging next to a cheap print of Martin Luther King, Jr., John Kennedy, and Robert Kennedy holding hands on a hilltop, staring at the clouds and an image of Jesus with open arms. The second hand swept toward twelve.

"Showtime," she said to herself as she hobbled across the room. She settled in front of a large television, her tired body fitting the contours of a red Naugahyde La-Z-Boy recliner. She picked up the remote control, aimed, and fired. A silver glow filled the darkness.

> *Good evening, Nashville. Welcome to the Scene at Ten. I'm Lisa Henson, along with Dave Rolander, bringing you the latest news from around Middle Tennessee. Tonight we have a special report on the mayor's proposal for a downtown arena. Also, part two in our series, "Drugs Invade The Schoolyard." Dave?*

> *Yes, Lisa. After sports and weather, we'll hear from our lifestyles reporter, Jonetta Jordan, who has been following Nashville's newest citizen, Hollywood mogul Mason Reed. Last night, Reed announced some big plans for Music City, and Jonetta was there.*

At the mention of Jonetta's name, Ethel Jordan's heart fluttered. Her love for her daughter was so deep and so strong, sometimes it scared her. Her pride in Jonetta scared her, too. She knew pride was the deadliest sin, but proud she was of her only child. Ethel was forty-two when she birthed Jonetta, and the baby's arrival was deemed miraculous by parents who had given up all hope of having children. In Ethel's mind, Jonetta had always been a child of destiny.

Finally, Jonetta appeared on the screen. Look at that smile, Ethel thought. Cost us a fortune. But, it worked, just like Joe said it would. He had usually been right about those things, rest his soul. Joe had always believed his daughter could do anything she set her mind to. Nothing was beyond her reach. And somehow, they had given her every advantage available: scrimping and saving to pay the orthodontist, the vocal coach, the dance teacher and tuition at Nashville's best private schools, all the way through Vanderbilt University, where, thankfully, she had received a full scholarship. Not bad for a black girl whose father had been a janitor. Too bad he didn't live to see her on *television*. Jonetta was wrapping up her report.

Last night we got further proof of Nashville's growing importance as a total entertainment center. Mason Reed, one of Hollywood's most powerful agents, announced his relocation here and his plans to turn "Music City" into "Movie City." He also unveiled his first Nashville-based production, "The Richard Petty Story," a film biography of the stock car racing legend, with, of course, a country music soundtrack. As if that weren't enough, Mr. Reed talked of a multi-million dollar soundstage and a new record company. His party at the Opryland Hotel was attended by hundreds of Music Row insiders and celebrities. There's definitely a major new player on the Nashville scene and his name is Mason Reed. This is Jonetta Jordan reporting for the Scene at Ten

After Jonetta's report, Ethel shook her head as if she had seen a vision. Though she had watched Jonetta hundreds of times, the experience still seemed wondrous to her, an uneducated woman raised on a sharecropper's farm in Alabama. Her only child, a star! Imagine that. At church, at the grocery, everywhere Ethel went, her friends and sometimes strangers would tell her how they admired Jonetta and how proud Ethel must be. *Oh, yes!* They would usually mention Oprah, another Nashvillian who had become a household name and rich beyond anybody's ability to calculate. Maybe someday Oprah could help Jonetta, they would suggest. But Ethel would politely remind them Jonetta was doing just fine on her own.

◆

Jonetta locked the door behind her and flicked on the room lamps. She took off her leather jacket and kicked her shoes across the room. After removing her wrap-around skirt and laying it across a chair, she stretched her hands above her head and then through her legs. At twenty-seven, she was still as limber as a dancer, and she hadn't gained a pound in ten years.

She walked to a sliding glass door, opened it and went out onto a small balcony overlooking the Cumberland River and downtown Nashville. She massaged her neck and contemplated the city. The January breeze was cold and stung her bare legs. She closed her eyes and took a deep breath. For a moment she was lost in a reverie—a little girl with a dog walking by a creek. She went back inside to the kitchen and poured herself a glass of milk, a lifelong habit. Mama was always giving her milk as a child. *For your teeth, baby, and your bones.* Mama. I better call her, Jonetta thought. She let the phone ring seven or eight times. She assumed Ethel had fallen asleep on the La-Z-Boy.

"Hello," said a sleepy voice.

"Hey, Mama, I'm home."

"You were good tonight, baby."

"You always say that."

"Only if it's true. If you weren't, I'd tell you."

"You better. Well, it's late and tomorrow is our shopping day. I'll pick you up around eleven. Okay?"

"I won't let you spend a lot of money on me."

"Whatever you say, Mama. Sweet dreams."

"Back 'atcha."

Jonetta smiled as she hung up. Then she saw the blinking light on her answering machine, a reminder of other people, most of them wanting something from her. She sighed and pressed Play.

Hey, baby. I made reservations at eight tomorrow night at Victor's per our discussion. I'll pick you up around seven-thirty. Please call and confirm. Bye. Her boyfriend, Charles, was the only black partner at the prestigious Nashville law firm Barkley and Stokes. They had been dating over two years and things were getting serious.

Beep.

Hello, Miss Jordan, this is A.J. Wilson. I represent the Silver Eagle Investment Group. A mutual friend gave me your name and I would like...

Fast forward.

Jonetta, this is Angela at Dr. Ballard's. It's time for your six month checkup. Please call to make an appointment.

Beep.

Hello. I, uh, I hope this is Jonetta Jordan's machine. Uh, my name is Tommy Price. You don't know me. I need to talk to you as soon as possible. I have some information that could be valuable to you. Very valuable. I'm sitting on something big. It concerns Mason Reed. I saw your report on him tonight and I think you would definitely be interested in this. This isn't a joke. Call me at 294----

She stopped the machine and shook her head. Damn, another weirdo. Maybe it's time for an unlisted number.

Two

It was over a year ago that Tommy Price had developed an intense crush on Jonetta. Whenever he could, he watched the ten o'clock news to catch a glimpse of her. He even recorded a series of her reports on his VCR in order to have a permanent copy of her image. On three occasions he had crashed music industry events where he hoped she might be. Once, at a Music Row block party, he was so close to her he could have touched her, but he didn't. He didn't dare. To him, she was a being from a higher plane of existence, beyond his reach. He knew it was silly, but that's how he felt.

Perhaps his loneliness fueled this unsettling infatuation with her. Or maybe she was the love of his life and they were destined to be together. He didn't know. But, as his feelings persisted month after month, he became concerned about himself. The whole thing was so irrational, so obsessive. Eventually, he sought help and spent several hundred scarce dollars on a psychiatrist. He wanted reassurance that he wasn't crazy, á la Hinckley. To his dismay, the doctor did not reassure him, but instead recommended they meet twice a week, indefinitely. Tommy's lack of health insurance and his stubborn refusal to ask his father for money, especially for a shrink, precluded therapy. But his friend, Gus, gave him some excellent, free advice. "Get to know her. Once you see she's human, like the rest of us, you'll get over it." Tommy knew he had to do something to burst the delusional bubble enveloping his head. Otherwise, he *would* go crazy. His strange experience with Mason Reed provided the perfect excuse to meet his fantasy. Now, he figured, he had something she would want—a scoop.

After several attempts Tommy finally talked to Jonetta and persuaded her to meet him. It wasn't easy, and when she said yes, he was surprised. They agreed on breakfast at the Pancake Pantry, a popular place with music biz types. He didn't like the choice of location, but she insisted. She told him she had never eaten there, which also surprised him. So the Pancake Pantry it was.

He was jumpy as he waited for her in a corner booth. Three cups of coffee hadn't helped his nerves. She was late and he wondered if she would show. He tapped his foot at least a hundred beats a minute and lit another cigarette. In two weeks Tommy would be twenty-six. He was skinny enough to cause some women to want to mother him. Sometimes that came in handy. Other women loved his curly, dark blonde hair. But his eyes were universally appreciated. He had his mother's eyes, ice blue, and he knew how to use them. Women liked Tommy Price.

When Jonetta entered the restaurant, he stubbed his cigarette and waved. As he had promised, he was wearing a red sweater. She spotted him and headed his way. He swallowed hard and tried to relax.

She extended her hand, all business. "I'm Jonetta Jordan."

"Tommy Price. I know this is unusual, but I think you'll be glad you came."

"I hope so. But, first things first. I'm starving."

"Can't beat the pancakes," he offered.

"So I've heard. Hey, is that Chet Atkins over there? At that back table?" She pointed behind Tommy.

"That's him. And he's sitting with Ray Stevens."

"You're right! Do you know them?" she asked hopefully.

Tommy shook his head, disappointed he couldn't make an introduction. "Sorry," he said.

"I thought you were in the music business, a songwriter," she said, kidding him.

"I am, but around here, who isn't?"

"I'm not."

"Count your blessings."

To his delight, Jonetta wanted to know about *him*. Credibility? He reeled off a quick biography, heavy on credibility. He was born and raised in Passaic, New Jersey, which he admitted was unlikely breeding ground for a country songwriter. His father was a lawyer; his mother was dead. His mother had grown up in South Carolina, where Tommy had lots of relatives, and he felt an affinity for the South. He had arrived in Nashville four years ago, soon after graduating from Rutgers with a "worthless" degree in philosophy. He had never had a song recorded but he had one on "hold" and he was hopeful.

"Define 'hold' for me," Jonetta said.

"It's like an option. You're not supposed to play the song for anyone else. First, you get a hold, then, if you're lucky, you get a cut," Tommy explained.

"Do you get paid for a hold?"

"No way. When it comes to songs, Nashville is a buyers' market."

"So how do you get by?"

"Well, Miss Jordan..."

"Just call me JJ," she interrupted. "Everybody does."

Upon hearing this intimation of friendship, he felt a soft, warm explosion in his chest. He looked in her eyes and knew he had been right about her. She was good. She was real.

"Great. JJ it is. I'm glad you asked how I get by. It's a good way for me to tell you my story."

She reached for her handbag and pulled out a tape recorder.

"Please, no tapes. This is so crazy, I'm not sure I believe it myself. Just listen, okay?"

She hesitated. "Okay, no tape. I won't even take notes."

"Thanks." He lit a cigarette. "Wish I could quit these things," he said. She nodded patiently and waited for him to begin.

"A limo. That's how I get by. Driving a limo. I actually own the limo. Well, fifty percent of it, anyway. With my partner, Gus. We specialize in unusual requests. By that I mean long trips, weekly or monthly rental, around-the-clock service. Anything the other services don't do, we will. You see?"

"Got it."

"Well, the same night as Mason Reed's party I got a call about two in the morning from the Opryland Hotel. The late night concierge there is a buddy of mine named George something. He said he needed me pronto for an important guest who wanted to do a little sight-seeing. Quote, unquote."

"At two A.M.?"

"Yeah, that's what I thought. But George said money was no object, so I quoted him sixty an hour, with a two hour minimum. I told him the hotel had to guarantee it. See, I bill the hotel and they pass it on to the guest. He said he would call back, which he did in about three minutes. He told me where to pick up my ride and so on." Tommy paused and took a deep drag from his cigarette.

"Go on, I'm listening."

"Well, I headed out to the hotel. Took me about twenty minutes. When I got there, sure enough, my ride was waiting as planned. He waved at me and jumped in the back seat. I

9

could tell he was slightly drunk. He looked to be in his early forties. A little bald on top. Stocky. Nice wool overcoat. Since George had told me to be careful with him, I knew he wasn't your average Joe. I asked him where to, and he reached in his pocket for a piece of paper, read it and said, 'Club Metro on Fourth Avenue South'."

Jonetta stopped him. "Club Metro . . . that's a gay bar, isn't it?"

"Right. Which is okay by me. Whatever turns your crank. Anyway, we drove downtown to the Club Metro. Took about fifteen minutes. During the ride I heard him breathing real heavy. I thought maybe he was sick or something. It sounded like he was mumbling to himself. So I said, 'Sir, are you okay?' And he snapped back, 'Yeah, I'm okay, asshole. Just drive.' Excuse my language, but that's what he said. I could tell he was a tough cookie and I decided to mind my own business and keep my eyes open. Sometimes my customers like conversation but not this guy. He was a real jerk.

"When we got to the club, I parked across the street and he told me to wait. It was getting close to three A.M. by then. Really cold outside. I let the engine run for the heater and within fifteen minutes, hey, I'm like falling asleep, thinking what an easy gig. Well, about four-thirty, somebody woke me up banging on the hood of the limo. Scared the sh-- well, it scared me. It was the bouncer. He told me my ride had gotten into a fight and I better come get him. Great, I thought, I knew this was too easy. As we were talking, my ride came staggering back to the car. He had a busted lip. The bouncer opened the door and pushed him in. At this point, I assumed he wanted to return to the hotel, so I said, 'Sir, would you like to go back to the hotel?' I could tell he was in pain. I asked if he wanted to go to the hospital. No reply. I looked in the rear view mirror but I couldn't see him. I thought he had passed out . . ."

Jonetta stopped him. "Tommy, I've got to be somewhere in thirty minutes. Can you speed it up?"

"Sure, sorry. Anyway, on the way back to the hotel he started talking to himself, like he was having a conversation with someone else. It was really weird. He would say, 'Who the hell is Mason Reed?' and then, in a different voice, answer himself, 'Mason Reed is king of the hill. Goy wonder of Hollywood.' I remember that—goy wonder of Hollywood. I was thinking this guy was psycho. But what really caught my ear was the name, Hector Armadas. He said it several times. Hector Armadas."

"Armadas, the cocaine king?"

"Bingo. That's the man. He's worth billions. He has his own army, and he's responsible for hundreds of murders and kidnappings, including judges and prosecutors. He's a real monster."

"Right. But what did this guy you thought was Mason Reed..."

"Oh, I know it was Mason Reed."

"How can you be so sure?"

"Because I met with him two days ago and he offered me a job."

"A job?"

"Yeah, I told you I had a story. But I'm getting ahead of myself. The important thing is what Reed said about Armadas." Tommy paused for effect and leaned closer to Jonetta. "That night, in the back of my limo, I heard Reed say that he was going to buy country music with Hector's money. He said within five years they would control the whole thing."

"Hmmm. That's good stuff. What else happened?"

"I got Reed back to the hotel. He was real drunk. No one else was around, so I helped him to his room. I practically carried him. I got his key from him and as I opened the door to his room, he grabbed my face and tried to kiss me, with his mouth open! I almost gagged. I threw him down in the hall. He was crying and sniveling like a kid, saying he was so, so sorry. Saying he loved me! It was really pathetic. At that moment, the door across the hall opened and this nice looking blonde peeked out, saw what was going on, and said, 'Oh, my God!' In less than a minute she was out in the hall with nothing on but a bath robe, helping this freak into his room. I just stood there in the hall in a slight state of shock. She came back, and like nothing had happened, asked me, 'Do you have a card?' I said no, and she said 'Wait a minute!' She got a pen and paper from her room and took my name and number. I asked her if this guy was really Mason Reed, and she said yes. She explained that he had been under a lot of pressure and had had way too much to drink that night at his big welcome-to-Nashville party. Then she asked me how much he owed me and I explained it would be on his bill. She gave me a fifty as a tip and asked me to be a pal and keep the whole thing quiet."

"Did she introduce herself?"

"No, not that night. But about three days later, she called me and said she was Susan Glass, vice president of Mason Reed and Associates. She was real smooth. She thanked me for the professional way I had handled the situation. I could tell she was a little nervous. Then she asked me if he had said or done anything that might be compromising. That was the word she used, 'compromising.' I told her I had taken him to a gay bar, if that's what she meant. And then, like an idiot, I told her about Hector Armadas."

"And?"

"Well, it was interesting. I heard her take a quick breath, like a gasp. Then there was a moment of silence. Finally, she laughed and said, 'That's a real whopper.' She said Mr. Reed had problems with grandiose thinking—exacerbated by drinking. In fact, she said he was under the care of a doctor. I thought that was a strange thing for her to admit."

"Anything else?"

"Yeah. There's more. She asked me about myself, my business. I told her I was a songwriter, moonlighting with the limo service. She said, 'Perfect, just perfect.' She was new in town and wanted to meet songwriters and learn about the scene. Then, out of the blue, she asked me out."

"A date?"

"Yeah, that was a first for me. Of course, she said it was business. But it got friendly fast."

"What do you mean?" Jonetta asked.

Bad move. Tommy didn't want to admit he had been intimate with Susan Glass on their first "date" and had enjoyed the most incredible sex with a woman he hardly knew or cared about. He didn't want to admit that, especially to Jonetta. "Well, uh, I mean she took a real personal interest in me and in my career. She listened to my songs. I told her about my plans, my dreams, and then, two days ago, it happened."

"What happened?"

"I met with Reed, and he offered me a job as creative director of his music publishing companies. At a *thousand* a week."

"Just like that?"

"Yeah, just like that."

"What did you tell him?"

"I said I needed some time to think about it. I . . ." Tommy hesitated.

"You what?"

"I wanted to talk it over with you."

"With me?"

"Yeah."

"Why?"

"I trust you."

"You don't even know me."

"I feel like I do. Anyway, you cover the music business. This could be a big story."

"Sure, if it's true. I have to be very careful. You've heard of libel?"

"Of course. I'm not stupid."

"I didn't say that, Tommy. But you're making some pretty serious charges. Before I get involved I need a lot more evidence than one drunken conversation."

"I realize that. So maybe I should take the job. You know, get inside. Plus, I could sure use the money."

"Maybe so. That's entirely up to you. But be careful, and please, keep me informed. Promise?"

"Promise."

A man with long, silver hair walked up behind Jonetta. He was wearing a faded denim jacket, scant protection from the sub-freezing weather. His frame was lanky and he moved with a loose-jointed gait. On a street corner he might have been mistaken for a panhandler, except that he held his head high and his strong chin out. He placed a large, rough hand on Jonetta's shoulder. She jumped an inch.

Tommy spoke. "Jonetta Jordan, meet Gus Rogers, my best friend, my partner in PNR Limousine Service, and one of Nashville's best songwriters. Though he keeps it a secret."

Gus flashed a winning grin. "Mornin' ma'am. Pleased to meet you. I've seen you on TV and you do a fine job, real fine."

Jonetta's heart was pounding from the startle Gus had given her. "Thank you," she said. "I was just about to go. Tommy has been telling me quite a story. Have you heard it?"

14

"At least a dozen times. Sounds about right. This town is ripe for a pluckin'. Dirty money has always been a part of the music business. So, nothing surprises me anymore." Gus chuckled.

"When it comes to people," Tommy added.

"Right, when it comes to people," Gus said and smiled.

"Amen," Jonetta said as she rose to leave. She gave Tommy her business card and made him promise, again, to stay in touch.

After she had left, Gus looked at Tommy and said, "I see what you mean. She's a class act."

Then, the waitress came to their table and Gus said to her, "Rachel, I swear you get better looking all the time."

Rachel frowned and said, "Oh, hush up, old man. You're just losing your eyesight!"

As Tommy watched their flirting, unexpected tears filled his eyes, which he quickly wiped away before Gus could see.

Three

That winter Nashville was a dismal place. For days at a time, the low sun disappeared, hidden by layers of drab clouds, and when moist, frigid air settled on the city, it generated an epidemic of colds and flu. On this bleak day, Tommy was suffering from his third sinus infection of the season. He had ingested antibiotics, squirted nasal spray, and inhaled steam, but relief was short-lived and recovery elusive. He was as miserable as the January weather. He stood in his tiny, drafty kitchen sipping orange juice. He was wearing the green robe his mother had given him for Christmas a month before she died. It was her last gift to him.

Tommy was worried. The limo, his sole source of income, required attention. According to Gus, the universal joint was "damn near shot" and the transmission needed an overhaul. Tommy dreaded the embarrassment of stranding an important customer while he flagged down assistance. He knew such a scenario was inevitable unless the Cadillac was serviced, but how? PNR's account was overdrawn and his credit cards maxed out. In these matters his partner was no help. Gus Rogers had been without money so long it seemed he had forgotten how the stuff worked. He operated strictly on a cash basis, which meant at any given time he might have twenty dollars in his ragged wallet. That was just enough for his daily bare-bones: cigarettes, coffee, one decent meal, and a half pint of bourbon to soothe his nerves after sundown. When his rent came due, he would scramble for a few days and pay the landlord. Despite his poverty, he had managed to keep the same apartment close to Music Row for years. Gus hated moving so much he would hire on as day laborer just to make rent. Once, Gus had explained to Tommy that for him money was like a beautiful woman he pursued endlessly but halfheartedly, convinced he would never win her, but too proud to admit he couldn't.

As Tommy brooded, feelings of impotence, like greedy termites, nibbled at the foundations of his self-esteem. More and more, fear of his own mediocrity haunted him like a secret disease. Before coming to Nashville, he had been confident, almost cocky, quite sure he was destined for big things. High school had been a breeze for him, and he had barely broken a sweat in college. But four years of rejection from the music business had taken a profound toll. Lately, when he looked in the mirror, he detected an unfamiliar sadness in his eyes. If he was wearing his chauffeur's cap and he studied himself, the effect was even sadder. Driving a limo did not jibe with his ambitions, and he was desperate to improve his lot in life.

He went to the refrigerator for more orange juice. As he reached for the door handle, he saw two business cards held fast by the same magnet. He put down his glass and removed the cards. *Jonetta Jordan, Lifestyles Reporter, WPIA, Channel Six.* That card was beige, cut from heavy stock, and the print was plain. He smiled as he remembered Jonetta. God, she was beautiful. A woman like that would never go for a loser. But, she was definitely interested in his tale about Reed. The other card was the one Susan Glass had given him. It was fancier than Jonetta's, and he assumed it was probably the most expensive card available. The finely detailed scroll print was embossed and the paper was almost transparent. Tommy closed his eyes and moved his forefinger across the raised lettering. He read it like braille, trying to divine some hidden meaning from the feel of the card itself. A thousand a week. That was more than his father paid third year associates! At that moment he decided to accept the job Reed had offered him. Tommy was ready to make a move, even a wrong one. If Reed was a gangster he would soon find out and Jonetta would be the next to know. Either way, he couldn't lose. As Tommy pressed Susan's number on his portable phone, he felt like he was entering a code which would open a gate to a new and dangerous world.

Four

Sonny Boy McDaniel had a problem. At the age of thirty-six, he had reached a crossroads in his career and his life. If he didn't break the top ten with his next single, he would probably lose his record deal, and in that event, he would, in short order, lose his bookings, then his booking agent, then his band and, most likely, within a year or so, his young wife, Tina (number three). Tina, in turn, would use her intimate knowledge of his "personal problems" to extort a substantial divorce settlement from him, and thus, he would lose what was left of his money.

Money. He shook his head and smiled wistfully. It always comes down to money. A wise head told him long ago, "The Nashville sound is really the ringing of the cash register." Lately, country music had never been bigger, and he wanted to get his while the getting was good. Hell, he thought, I've sacrificed my whole existence to entertaining the "friends and neighbors," as he derisively referred to country music fans. If he could just get on a roll, he would roll right out of Nashville, down to the Caribbean and an early retirement.

Twenty years of endless touring had cured him of any romantic notions about show business. He had hit the concert trail when he was sixteen, dropping out of high school to join his mother's show as "Sonny Boy," teenage wonder, little more than a mascot. In his mind, he was a well paid carney, a circus performer, a southern-fried freak of nature. Despite years of therapy with several of Nashville's best professional listeners, he remained desperately unhappy.

It wasn't easy being the only child of Ruby McDaniel, one of the bona fide greats in country music. She was the first woman to sell a million singles, "If You're Thinking 'Bout Leavin', Leave the Thinking to Me," (1959); the first woman inducted into the Country Music Hall of Fame (1962); and the first woman in Tennessee to be ordered to pay alimony (Charlie Miner, 1967).

Sonny Boy squirmed on the plush, overstuffed waiting room sofa and looked down at another problem, his expanding belly. In the last few years, he had picked up a couple dozen pounds from a relentless and almost unavoidable diet of fatty road food. American Records had informed him through the kind offices of Patty Carter, head of A&R, that he had to lose "at least twenty pounds, shoot for thirty, big boy." If he did not, Patty had warned him, American would not advance the fifty thousand dollars plus required to produce a video. Without a video, his single's chances were nil.

Sonny Boy knew one sure-fire way to lose twenty pounds. Quickly. No dieting. No exercise. His nose tingled with a Pavlovian reflex, a muscle memory of the magical white powder. His face started to flush. He gripped the arm of the couch and took a deep breath. Breathe in on three, out on six. In on three, out on six. His panic eased as a sixtyish woman in a severe gray suit appeared at the door of the waiting room.

"Your mama's got a minute now," she said. Mavis Herndon smiled at Sonny Boy in a knowing way which implied a mutual understanding. Mavis had been at Ruby's side longer than anyone. They had grown up together in Jasper, Mississippi, on the same street in identical row houses built by the paper manufacturer which had employed both their daddies at subsistence wages. When Ruby left for Nashville, Mavis was right behind her.

Mavis knew Ruby was a star the first time she saw her

holding forth to a gaggle of barefooted children on a dusty Jasper street, belting out "You Are My Sunshine." By the time Ruby was fourteen, she wore enough makeup (in the daytime!) to embarrass a hooker, scandalizing her Primitive Baptist family and providing Mavis with vicarious participation in Ruby's rebellion.

"Mavis, someday I'm gonna be a star! You watch. I got my mind set on it," Ruby would say. Then, Mavis would nod her head in solemn approval, awed by her friend, amazed that a girl from Jasper, Mississippi, could really believe she would amount to anything more than a working man's wife and a put-upon mother.

Ruby and Mavis had grown up poor, dirt poor, as they liked to say. Poor was a feeling deep in their bones. On distant summer nights, they had lain on blankets under the stars and talked for hours about all the things they would buy and places they would go when they were R-I-C-H. The very sounds of those words—New York, maids, minks, pearls, Hollywood, air conditioning, silk, Cadillacs, diamonds, Paris, swimming pools—were so powerful that just saying them out loud made them dizzy. When Mavis was sixteen, her mother died from an infection that wouldn't have killed her had she received proper medical treatment, and at that moment Mavis turned with all her being and bonded herself to Ruby, who became her source of strength and hope. Since then, they had been inseparable, and through it all, their friendship endured and deepened.

Sonny Boy noticed Mavis' large bottom as he followed her down the hall. Mavis has added some pounds herself, he thought. But, he loved Mavis. Mavis had parented him at least as much as Ruby, and they were, the three of them, a family. Through the years he had heard the ugly talk that Ruby and Mavis were more than friends. But he knew such scandal wasn't so. For one thing, Ruby's weakness for men was well documented through her five marriages, two of which were to the same man, Sonny Boy's father, the late Elmo McDaniel. She always had a man on call, usually a wannabe singer many years her junior. About Mavis he wasn't so sure. He considered her asexual, despite his doubts that anybody could do without "it," in whatever form "it" came.

Mavis opened an ornate oak door, inlaid with a hand-carved scene of a pioneer woman standing in front of a Conestoga wagon, peering courageously into a valley. He entered a large room choked with memorabilia from Ruby's career. At one end of the room, there was a stone fireplace with a black kettle in the hearth. On the mantle sat Ruby's most prized possession, her Grammy for best country album, What Every Woman Knows, 1962. Gold records, citations, photographs, sheet music and magazine covers fought with each other for space on the walls. The hardwood floor was covered with an antique Navajo rug.

Sonny Boy felt a tightness in his chest as he walked the long room toward his mother. The walls seemed to draw around him with suffocating force. He felt like he was walking through liquid.

At her desk, Ruby was writing furiously on a note pad. She wore a powder blue jump suit with a fur-trimmed collar and sleeves. Her hands were adorned with seven rings, each containing her birthstone, the ruby. He stopped in front of the desk and looked at her, admiring her total self-immersion and her concentration on the task before her.

"Well, take a seat and stay a spell," she said without looking up.

He sat in one of the two wingback chairs facing her massive desk, which had been fashioned from one giant slab of cypress, a gift from the state of Florida in gratitude for Ruby's hurricane relief efforts. Finally, she put down her golden pen and looked at him, removing her rhinestone-studded reading glasses. For a frozen moment, they looked at each other, without apparent emotion but with an eerie intensity, like a person might study himself in a mirror.

"Are you clean?" she asked in a whisper, with a profound sense of seriousness.

He looked at the top of his snakeskin boots. Then he looked her in the eye. "Clean as a whistle."

She permitted herself a slight smile and said, "One day at a time."

"One day at a time," he repeated, mantra-like. Another long silence passed between them as if they were communicating telepathically.

"Well, what's on your mind, son?" she said, meaning what do you want?

"I've got problems, Ruby." When Sonny Boy wanted to talk business he called his mother by her name, which was appropriate, since she also served as his manager, for ten percent of his gross earnings, half the going rate. She waited for him to elaborate.

"Patty Carter wants me to lose a little weight before she'll commit to a video," he said.

"Patty's right, Sonny. You're getting fat! And TV adds ten. Why don't you just make up your mind and do it? Eat less and exercise more. Count fat grams, you know the score."

"Mama, I've tried and tried to lose weight. It's the damn road and all those grease pits. You know, Mama, I truly believe I'm twenty pounds away from a hit."

Suddenly, Ruby became impatient. "Is that why you came here? To tell me you need to lose some weight? Hell, everybody in town knows that."

For once in his life Sonny Boy did not wither under his mother's sarcasm. He shot right back at her, "No. I'm here 'cause I'm gonna go see Mason Reed tomorrow. And if Mason Reed wants to represent me, I'm inclined to say yes, let's go, let's do it."

Ruby sank back in her chair. "He'll take twenty percent."

"Mama, you know what they say about percentages. If he can earn it, fine. Maybe he'll pay you an override. The truth is I need a whole new thing. A new career plan. You're so close, you can't see me. We've done good but I'm thirty-six years old and I'm still bubbling under! It's now or never for me."

"What about American?"

"Well, what about American? They can either get on board or get off. Anyway, this guy is starting his own record label and he's looking for somebody like me. Somebody with a name who hasn't peaked yet. That's me, by God!"

Ruby got up from her desk and walked to the window, lost in thought. Finally she asked, "And just who is this Mason Reed I've heard so much about? You gotta be careful who you turn your life over to."

Sonny Boy could sense his mother coming around. "He's *only* one of the three or four most powerful guys in show business. He moved here from L.A. Gonna do it all. Even movies," he said.

"Well, why is he coming to little ole Nashville if he's such a big shot in Hollywood?"

"The other night at the Opryland Hotel he said he'd been thinkin' about it for years. He thinks the future is here. He said he loves country music and wants to take it worldwide." Sonny Boy's voice dropped a notch. "Look, Mama. I've checked this guy out. He's the real deal. He might be my last chance. I just want your permission to talk to him."

Ruby smiled weakly. "I appreciate that, son. You coming here first." She crossed the room and pointed at a framed *Billboard* country chart. "See that. October 26, 1959. Number one. 'If You're Thinking 'Bout Leavin', Leave the Thinking to Me.' A million singles. Without that, I'd be slinging hash at a diner, and God knows where you'd be. The truth is, with me and with American you've never had a number one. Without a hit, you're nothing. If Mason Reed can get you a hit, then you've got more than my permission, you've got your mama's blessing."

Sonny Boy smiled and thought, sometimes she really comes through, God bless her.

Ruby continued, "But with or without Mason Reed, you better lose some weight, if for no other reason than your health."

Sonny Boy laughed. "Okay, Mama. It's a deal. And one more thing, thanks."

FIVE

Mason Reed and Associates occupied the top floor of the new twelve-story Crown Tower, in the heart of Music Row. "Music Row" was actually two one-way streets, Sixteenth and Seventeenth Avenues, which ran parallel in opposite directions. Along both streets, homes built before World War II had been converted to offices for music publishing companies, production companies, attorneys, managers and booking agents. The large international record labels had constructed their own sleek office buildings scattered among the painted brick cottages. The hodgepodge architectural jumble seemed quaint, but inside those offices, the stakes were high.

As Sonny Boy was ushered into Mason's office by Susan Glass, two things struck him. First, Mason Reed had an incredible view of downtown Nashville and the surrounding green hills. Second, there was no Mason Reed in the office.

"Where's the man?" he asked Susan.

"Just make yourself comfortable. He'll make his entrance momentarily." With that assurance, she excused herself.

Sonny Boy surveyed the room, which seemed to him sterile and empty, especially compared to his mother's flea market of an office. Everything was clean, cool, and modern, from the marble desk and chrome chairs to the strange cubistic painting behind the black leather couch. He didn't see a single photograph, award, memento: not a piece of evidence which might provide a clue to the occupant's character or personality. The office reminded him of the one belonging to that shrink he saw when he had lived in Atlanta, during one of his failed attempts to escape Nashville. As he sat down he noticed a dying ficus tree in the corner.

Then, a hidden door, disguised as a full length mirror, opened and Mason Reed appeared. He was shorter than Sonny Boy had expected, maybe a little shy of five seven. But he was powerfully built, and Sonny Boy thought he must pump iron to get that kind of upper body development. Mason moved quickly, darting from the door to behind his desk as if in one motion. Sonny Boy rose and extended his hand.

"Sonny Boy McDaniel at your service," he said brightly.

Mason did not extend his hand but said, "Please forgive me. I don't *do* handshakes. Did you know that a majority of colds and flus are transmitted by the hands? I just can't afford to get sick. But trust me, I know who you are and I'm very pleased to meet you."

Sonny Boy was a little taken aback at Mason's refusal to shake hands, but quickly dismissed it as flaky Hollywood behavior. Mason, still standing, turned his back to Sonny Boy and faced the panorama of Nashville.

"Sonny Boy, big, big things lie ahead for this city, for this community. And, damnit, it *is* a community. People know each other here. They care about each other. It's not like L.A. What an emotional wasteland! Community is why I came here. I made the most important career move of my life when I moved to Nashville. And why did I do it? Community, damnit, that's why. Community!" He paused. "But also, Sonny Boy, the times they are a-changin', in the immortal words of Bobby Dylan. Indeed, they are a-changin'. And fast. He who hestitates is lost. Lost! Out of luck! An also-ran! A schmuck! You see, in the first half of the century, it was New York, New York. If I can make it there, etcetera, etcetera. After World War II, L.A. replaced New York as the center from which pop culture emerged, flowed, gushed. But the next century belongs to the American heartland, and Nashville is the capital of the heartland! Don't you see? This country is seeking its psychic center and it's here! Maybe Nashville is corny, maybe it's square, but I'm telling you, we're STANDING IN THE PSYCHIC CENTER OF THIS COUNTRY! And the psychic center of this country is actually the PSYCHIC CENTER OF THIS PLANET. Right? Of course, I'm right, damnit." Mason stopped and turned slightly to see if Sonny Boy was on board his train of thought. Sonny Boy was enthralled. He nodded weakly.

Mason continued, "I had a vision, a mystical vision, about this place. It hit me at the moment that seven pointer knocked me out of bed. Just kidding. I had a vision, hell, let me rephrase that. I *have* a vision! And when a man has a vision he can see where he's going. And when he can see where he's going he'll get there if he never stops. And when he gets there he'll have thousands of jerks behind him who don't have, never had, and never will have a VISION!" Mason took a breath and wiped away a drivel of spit from the side of his mouth. Then he turned to Sonny Boy, leaned across his desk, pointed his finger at Sonny Boy's nose, and shouted, "Elmo Donald McDaniel, Jr., DO *YOU* HAVE A VISION?" How does he know my full name, Sonny Boy was thinking when Mason boomed even louder, "I said, SONNY BOY McDANIEL, DO *YOU* HAVE A VISION?"

Sonny Boy tried to collect his thoughts and stammered, "Yeah, I, uh, I guess I have a, yeah, sure, a vision. I have a vision. I do. At least, a vision of me. I mean for me."

"What is your vision?"

Sonny Boy responded evenly and deliberately, "A number one record in *Billboard* magazine, with my name right beside it. That's it. That's my vision."

Mason smiled at the modesty of Sonny Boy's vision. "Well, that's a start." Then he pressed the intercom. "Susan, bring in Mr. McDaniel's file."

File? Where does this guy get off having a file on me? Sonny Boy asked himself. Mason Reed was making Sonny Boy angry. He tried to calm himself with his breathing exercises. In on three, out on six. In on three, out on six. Susan appeared with the file, handed it to Mason, and as she turned, she winked at Sonny Boy. He relaxed a little.

"Mr. Reed, if you don't mind me asking..."

"Always ask. It's the only way you learn," Mason said, his voice coated with condescension.

"Right. Why do you have a file on me, and what does it contain? I think I'm entitled to know. After all, we're not in business together. I don't recall giving you permission..."

"Wait a minute, country boy. We are ALL in business together. All of us. The whole damn world is in business together. That's what life is... business. And since I am en-ter-tain-ing the prospect of rep-re-sent-ing you, first I'm gonna check you out thoroughly. And guess what?"

"What?"

"I don't like what I see," Mason said coldly.

Sonny Boy was startled at this naked display of cruelty, accustomed as he was to fans, flunkies, and sycophants. "You don't like what you see?" Sonny Boy asked meekly.

Like a coil, Mason sprang to his feet, turned to face the window, and delivered a blistering monologue. "Sonny Boy McDaniel. Only child of the great Ruby McDaniel, a member of the Country Music Hall of Fame, and the late, not-so-great Elmo D. McDaniel, a no-count drunk who blew his head off..."

"Hey, wait a minute, mister."

"He blew his head off after your mother left him. For the

second time, I see. Poor bastard. I guess he didn't like being the *wind beneath her wings*. A real loser. A coward. He left you to be raised by Ruby and," he referred to the file, "one Mavis Herndon, who may or may not be your mother's lesbian lover."

"No way, man!" Sonny Boy was on his feet, and at that moment, he wanted to tear Mason apart.

"Like I said, may or may *not* be your mother's lover. But back to the subject at hand, Sonny Boy McDaniel. I see you were kicked out of three boarding schools, including two military schools. Didn't like the uniform, did ya big boy? So you go to work for mama at sixteen, opening her shows. Not much of a life for a teenager, was it? Tough way to grow up. Maybe that's why you've had such a hard time with drink and drugs and drugs and more drugs! According to this report, you've tried 'em all. It appears you like the chemicals, especially cocaine. And, let's see, married three times, including the present Mrs. McDaniel, the former Tina Weathers, Miss Dallas 1990. Nineteen years old when you made her an honest woman. Just a baby, Sonny Boy!" Mason shot a glance at McDaniel, going for the kill. "According to my sources, Miss Dallas is screwing your drummer, one Jerry Suddath. Why don't you fire him? I guess good drummers are hard to come by!"

Mason let out a fiendish cackle, and Sonny Boy felt a wave of nausea sweep over him. Finally, he could take no more. He grabbed Mason by the lapel.

"Hey, you sonavabitch, I don't know what circle of hell you came from, but if you don't stop airing my dirty laundry like you're getting off on it, I'm gonna tear your face off!" Sonny Boy surprised himself at the fury in his voice.

Mason's mercurial demeanor changed instantly. His face relaxed and took on a beatific appearance. He sat down, raised his hand and said gently, "Relax, my friend. You have just experienced the famous Mason Reed shock treatment. I only wanted to get your attention."

Sonny Boy was so thoroughly beside himself he couldn't speak. He felt his heart pounding. This man had extracted such an intense emotional response from him, he actually wanted to *kill* Mason Reed. He had never felt that way before.

"Please sit down and relax," Mason cooed. "Take a deep breath. Would you like a drink? A beer? A little wine? I've got an incredible collection of California cabernets..."

"No! Hell no! Look Reed, if you don't convince me in the next three minutes that you're not psycho, I'm gonna walk outta here and tell everybody I know in this town, and I know everybody in this town worth knowing, that you're the slimiest piece of scum that ever washed up on the shore..."

Sonny Boy stopped as Mason handed him a check. It was made out to Elmo D. McDaniel, Jr., p.k.a. Sonny Boy Mc-Daniel, drawn on the account of Mason Reed and Associates in the amount of five hundred thousand dollars.

"What's this?" Sonny Boy demanded.

"It's a check, dimwit. A signing bonus. Not a loan, not an advance. And it sure ain't a gift. No tricks. It's yours if you sign with me. Susan has the contract ready. But listen to me, cowboy. Every major change we make in the contract at your request, we deduct fifty thousand from the bonus. You keep the half mill only if we don't make any material amendments to the contract as presented to you. Only I, and I alone will decide what constitutes a material amendment. So, when you take the contract to your lawyer, and I *urge* you to do so, remember the formula. And..." Mason paused. "You'll have a number one record within two years. If not, I pay you another half million and the deal terminates. It's all in the contract. Now, give me the check back. It's not yours... yet."

At that moment Sonny Boy was totally flustered. He really wasn't sure of his surroundings. His head was spinning and his stomach was churning. Susan arrived to escort him from the room.

"I want a reply within a week," Mason barked. "Remember, I've got 'em lined up to see me. Consider yourself lucky."

On his way out, Sonny Boy saw John Farley Stringer in the waiting room. John Farley and Sonny Boy exchanged furtive glances, choosing not to acknowledge each other. Sonny Boy had heard recently that John Farley was being dropped from Atlantic Records, his last album having sold less than fifty thousand units. Sonny Boy smiled at the thought of Stringer, whom he had never liked, undergoing Mason's shock treatment. He also clutched the package containing his contract a little tighter.

Six

Mavis poured two jiggers of Glenfiddich scotch into a heavy Waterford tumbler. One cube of ice. Every evening after work she made drinks for herself and Ruby, who preferred a dry vodka martini up with two large Spanish olives and a twist. Their cocktail hour provided some quiet time for summing up the day's events and plotting tomorrow's strategy. Mavis stirred her drink with her forefinger as she considered the question posed to her by Ruby: What did she make of this character, Mason Reed? Mavis didn't answer, pondering the situation as she returned to her chair.

Ruby continued, "Sonny Boy said Reed was pretty rough on him. Has a file full of real personal stuff. He said the guy promised him a number one record within two years, in writing! That sounds fishy to me. How can he do that? And of course, the kicker is that check for a half a million dollars, which would turn anybody's head. It's hard to argue with five hundred grand. *That* much money would solve a lot of problems for Junior. Maybe he could pay off Tina and get her out of his life. I begged him not to marry that tramp. But you know men—two-headed monsters who can't think with either one. Anyway, my sources tell me Tina's been shacking up with Jerry Suddath."

"Who is Jerry Suddath?" Mavis asked.

"Sonny's new drummer, for God's sake."

"Ain't it always the drummer?" Mavis replied.

They both giggled. Several moments of silence passed before Ruby resumed her stream of consciousness regarding

Sonny Boy's dilemma. "I don't know what else to do for the boy, Mavis. Listen to me now, calling him a boy! He's a thirty-six-year-old man. My daddy was forty-four when he died, and I thought he was an old man. I'll tell you one thing, I never doubted my daddy *was* a man. I just don't know about Sonny. In some ways he's had it too easy. In other ways, he's had it real hard."

Ruby didn't have to elaborate. Elmo's suicide when Sonny Boy was seven was the single most painful memory that Ruby had to carry, and Mavis knew it. Mavis spoke softly, "I have observed that the children of suicides have a rough row to hoe. But Ruby, you've done your best by Sonny. He knows you were there for him. He knows you're still there for him. If you spoiled him a little, so be it. Maybe it's time he was out there on his own, with or without Mason Reed."

"Oh, I'm resigned to losing him as a client. Really, in a way I'm relieved. But how can Reed promise a number one record, in writing?"

"Two ways," Mavis said firmly. "Either the promise isn't worth the paper it's written on or..."

"Or what?"

"Or, if he actually intends to deliver, it'll take money, and lots of it. Good old-fashioned payola."

Payola was not a word spoken lightly in polite music industry circles, but Mavis and Ruby knew that the practice of paying deejays and program directors to play a record was as old as radio itself, and they assumed it was as current as today's top ten.

Ruby reflected. "Do you remember when Charlie drove all night up to Detroit to buy that deejay? I think that station cost us a whopping seventy-five dollars. They added my record the next morning, right before the *Billboard* reports were due. That one station saved my bullet. Without it, who knows? I always loved Charlie for that. Best money we ever spent."

Mavis remembered. "Amen, sister. I always liked ol' Charlie, too. He was loyal."

"But dumb as a brick!" Ruby said.

"Not too dumb to get three years of alimony out of you," Mavis reminded her.

Ruby ignored Mavis' jibe. She returned to the subject of payola instead. "I wonder what a *Billboard* station would cost today?"

"Heaven knows. Considering inflation, probably seventy-five hundred," Mavis answered matter-of-factly.

"Well, I've had enough worrying 'bout it. It's time for Sonny Boy to move on. We never got him a hit. We came close, but this ain't horseshoes. American is ready to drop him. Mason Reed might be his last shot. I vote yes on Reed." With that, she turned up her martini, drained it, took out the olives and popped one in each side of her mouth.

"I'm not so sure, Ruby. I smell a rat. Mason Reed is a carpetbagger. An opportunist. He doesn't know country music. My guess is he doesn't even like country music. He looked over the fence, saw the grass was greener, and bought himself a big fancy riding lawnmower. If he buys Sonny Boy a hit, that'll be all it is—bought and paid for. The people won't give a damn about it. What Junior needs is a great song. Good songs are a dime a dozen but great songs are few and far between. As for your involvement, I say either way, let him go. It's time. He's gotta stand on his own, if he can. If he can't, it might do him good to get down on his knees."

As usual, Mavis made a lot of sense. Suddenly Ruby felt light as a feather. She realized her days as her son's manager were over. Whether he turned his life over to Mason Reed, Joe Schmo, or Jesus Christ was beyond her control. Ruby's natural optimism returned along with her appetite.

"Let's eat out tonight, Mavie!"

"Sure, what sounds good?"

"Japanese. I've got a jones for some crunchy shrimp rolls."

"Japanese it is." Then Mavis raised her glass. "Here's to Junior, may the Lord bless and keep him."

Ruby raised her empty glass. "To Junior, and a number one record!"

SEVEN

Whenever Jonetta was troubled with a difficult decision, she didn't hesitate to rely on her mother's fundamental wisdom. Despite Ethel's lack of education, Jonetta considered her a shrewd judge of character and an accurate assessor of circumstance. Ethel was the person Jonetta trusted most.

The phone rang several times before Ethel answered. Jonetta imagined Ethel shuffling from the La-Z-Boy to the phone, hobbled by arthritic knees.

"H'lo."

"Mama, it's Jonetta."

"Hey, baby girl. How you doing?"

"Fine, just fine. But I've got something heavy on my mind. I need a little advice."

"Okay sweetie. Let me sit down and put on my thinking cap. Go ahead on."

"Mama, I've met a young man..."

"What about Charles?"

Jonetta knew her mother liked Charles. "No, Mama, not *that* kind of man. This fellow has a story to tell. It's about the music business. It involves some real bad people moving into Nashville, trying to take over country music."

"Well, I don't know much about country music, Jonetta."

"I don't either, Mama. There aren't a lot of black faces in country music..."

"Charley Pride!"

"Right. He's about the only one. I've tried for years to get inside the country music crowd. But they're pretty cliquish on Music Row. Anyway, this young man, a songwriter, tells me that the people who sell cocaine want to buy their way into Nashville."

"Honey, you know how I feel about that cocaine. It's a plague. Evil stuff. Why, last week Mildred Thompson, do you remember Mildred?"

"Yes, I think so. Didn't she live cattycorner to Mitchum's Market?"

"That's right. Well, last week Mildred's grandson, Chucky, was murdered in a drug deal in Chicago. All over cocaine, or crack, or whatever they call it. Lord have mercy, it tore down poor Mildred. She can't get out of the bed she's so heartsick. Cocaine is the devil's tool!"

"I know, Mama, and I agree. That's the main reason I want to follow this story. But Mama..."

"Yes, child?"

"I'm scared, Mama. These are real bad people."

"What about the police?" Ethel suggested.

"I don't have enough evidence yet. I need to investigate more before I go to the authorities. If I'm wrong, it could hurt my credibility."

"Jonetta, just remember what your daddy always told you," Ethel advised.

"I know, Mama. 'You can never go wrong as long as you do the right thing.'"

"That's right, JJ. 'You can never go wrong as long as you do the right thing.' Problem always is, knowing what's right! You pray on it and I'll pray on it and in His good time the Lord will show you the way. Then it's up to you to follow His lead... wherever it takes you."

Jonetta listened intently, like a child hearing a bedtime story. She envied her mother's simple but unshakable faith. "Well, Mama, do pray for me, okay? That makes me feel good, knowing that you'll be praying for me."

"I will baby, and if you want me to, I'll add your name to our prayer chain." Ethel belonged to a group of women who prayed daily for a list of needy, sick, and troubled souls.

"Yes ma'am, please do that. Add my name to the prayer chain. Ask them to help me know the right thing to do. But, my goodness, enough 'bout me. How are you feeling?"

"Oh, child, I'm fine 'cept for these rickety knees. I wish I could trade 'em in for a new pair."

"I just read about a new arthritis medicine. It's supposed to be a miracle drug," Jonetta said hopefully.

"I could use a miracle for these old legs."

"Mama, I'll pray for your miracle and you pray for mine, okay?"

"Okay."

"Bye-bye."

"Bye-bye angel."

After she hung up, Jonetta allowed herself to ponder how much she cherished her mother. What will I do when she passes? What will I do?

EIGHT

He felt a burning sensation in his stomach, like a hot knife had entered his gut. He let out a pathetic moan, but his pain elicited no sympathy from the man behind him.

"Come on, don't wimp out! Give me ten more," a voice demanded sternly.

Sonny Boy strained to perform another situp on the incline bench as beads of perspiration stung his eyes. He was three weeks into a rigorous exercise and diet regimen designed to trim thirty pounds from his frame and make him more "video friendly." After completing three more situps with great effort, Sonny Boy went limp. He felt the blood rushing to his brain and his pulse pounding in his ears.

"Jesus, Ricky. I'm about to bust a gut! I've already done a hundred of these suckers. Gimme a break."

"Okay, boss. But you know what we have to do. Thirty pounds in two months. According to today's weigh-in, you've got twenty-one pounds to go. And less than five weeks to do it in. Let's hit the treadmill."

As Sonny Boy slowly and begrudgingly made his way to the treadmill, he glanced at the mirrors lining the gym. Perhaps it was wishful thinking, but he saw an improvement in his appearance. His belly was definitely flatter. He turned to his trainer. "You know, my contract originally specified *fifty* pounds in two months."

"Oh, man! Fifty pounds would be tough, maybe impossible," Ricky said sympathetically.

"Yeah, I know. That's why I made 'em change it. Of course, it cost me fifty grand. *A material amendment.*"

"Fifty grand? What do you mean?"

"Oh, it's a long story. Just one of Mason's clever tricks." In an odd way, Sonny Boy was enjoying his spartan routine. He even experienced a warm feeling toward Mason, but it passed quickly.

NINE

The cardboard box on Tommy's desk contained at least a hundred cassettes; each cassette carried three or four song titles. Tommy shook his head as he calculated the time required to review three or four hundred songs. And this box represented only one week's worth of submissions! Had he known the competition was this fierce, he would have never left New Jersey. As he rummaged through the tapes he saw a few names of songwriters he knew and the names of many he didn't know. All these people had submitted samples of their work to him in the hope of securing a staff position at Nashville's newest publishing company, the House of Reed, which Tommy was now running with limited assistance from a twenty-year-old college student named David Kraselsky, a fellow transplant from the North. He yelled for David, who quickly appeared in the doorway.

"Yo' boss?"

"David, I can't possibly listen to all these tapes and do everything else I've got to do. So, I'm going to go through this box and pick out the names I recognize as decent writers. The rest I'll give to you. If you hear anything interesting, bring it back to me. Okay?"

"Sure, but do I have to listen to every song on the cassette? Usually, you can tell from the first song."

Tommy realized this was not the first time Kraselsky had screened unsolicited material, one of the more thankless jobs on Music Row.

"Yeah, I know most of it is bad. But listen to the first

thirty seconds of every song, just in case there's a diamond in the dirt."

"Okay, boss, but it'll have to wait until tomorrow. I've got a class in twenty minutes."

"Sure, tomorrow's fine. Go ahead and split." What could Tommy expect from an unpaid intern earning course credit in Music Publishing 101 by working on the Row? Mason Reed seemed to throw money at the other divisions of his expanding empire, but when it came to the House of Reed, he was a tightwad. Tommy wondered why Reed bothered at all with a publishing company, given his lack of interest. Regardless, Tommy was glad to have the job. At least his salary was generous. Better yet, for the first time since he had arrived in Nashville driving his uncle's dying Chevrolet, he was on the "inside." When he walked the halls at the Crown Tower, he sensed the power seeping out from under all those closed doors. The place vibrated with intoxicating energy. Sometimes the effect of the buzz was almost hallucinatory.

Each week brought new arrivals from L.A. as big city go-getters flocked to Middle Tennessee. Tommy was intrigued by the people who seemed to be deserting Hollywood in a surging wave of talent, especially since a recent series of earthquakes. Locals mused that within days of a major shake in California, the phones in Nashville would light up with job inquiries from the West Coast. Tommy was beginning to believe Mason's propaganda that someday Nashville would succeed L.A. as the pop-cultural center of the country.

His dark doubts about Mason wouldn't go away, though, and he reserved a special place in his mind for them. But usually, he was so busy he had no time for anything other than the considerable task of building the House of Reed. He was learning all he could about contracts, copyrights, licenses, and royalties. The job also provided common ground with his father, who was thrilled at Tommy's good fortune in obtaining an executive position. Once or twice a week Tommy called his dad in Passaic to ask him a legal question or for general advice.

His father had never supported his move to Nashville in pursuit of such a foolhardy career as songwriting. He had been sorely disappointed when Tommy had turned his back on law school. The ensuing years seemed to justify his father's fears.

Before Mason Reed came along, Tommy had little to show for his efforts except hard-won experience and a budding cynicism. Now, he was making more money than his father paid third year associates, and he was working for a man *The Wall Street Journal* had profiled as a "turn of the century information age visionary." Mason had purchased PNR's limousine at a premium, hired Gus as his driver, and, at Tommy's insistence, signed Gus to an exclusive songwriter's agreement with the House of Reed. Lately, Gus had never seemed happier. He even looked ten years younger. All in all, Mason Reed was doing good things for PNR. As Gus said, "Laissez les bons temps roulet." *Let the good times roll.*

TEN

For some reason, Tommy Price kept popping up in Jonetta's thoughts. At the oddest times she found herself thinking of him. Resolved to do something about it, she decided to spend her precious lunch break in the television station's research room, seated in front of a computer.

She pulled up Passaic, New Jersey, and accessed its commercial telephone listings. The only Price listed as an attorney in Passaic was Evelyn B. Price. Then she entered Rutgers University and accessed its graduates. She got the Prices. In all its glorious history Rutgers had graduated two hundred and twenty-one Prices, seventeen of whom shared the name Thomas. Of these, seven were living, and Edward Thomas Price, class of '74, was the latest graduate. Obviously, that wasn't *her* Tommy Price.

At that point Jonetta had no choice but to doubt Tommy's veracity. About everything. Too bad. Nice guy. Great eyes. She knew he had taken the job with Mason Reed because she had seen a press release to that effect in *Billboard* over a month ago. But he hadn't called her as he had promised.

She went back to her desk hungry and grouchy from missing lunch. She ordered a club sandwich to be delivered and felt better knowing food was en route. She looked at the five by seven of Charles on her desk. He was so handsome. He had modeled occasionally, but the law firm discouraged it, and he had stopped when he made partner. In fact, she had first spotted Charles in a pajama ad in *The Tennessean*.

Through a contact at the newspaper she had gotten his name and, through another friend, arranged an introduction.

Tommy came into her mind again. Damn. She found the number for Mason Reed and Associates, called it, and asked for Thomas Price, the name used in the *Billboard* article. The receptionist put her through.

"Hello, this is Thomas Price," he said with a touch of formality.

"Tommy! Jonetta Jordan. Remember me? Congratulations on your new position."

"Hey, JJ! How ya' been? I'm sorry I haven't called. Really, you wouldn't believe how many times I've thought about you."

"So, why didn't you call me, like you promised?"

"Well, I guess the truth is, I was embarrassed."

"Embarrassed?"

"Yeah. Obviously, I took the job. And, so far, so good. No gangsters with Spanish names. I think I was under the influence of an overactive imagination." He paused. "In more ways than one."

"What do you mean by that?"

"Well, I, uh, I was, uh, attracted to you. Very much so. And I thought, maybe, you were attracted to me. At least, I hoped so."

"What?"

"Yeah. And I still think you're the most beautiful girl I've ever seen. There, I said it."

"I beg your pardon?"

"Look, I confess. I've been in love with you for a long time. I can't stop thinking about you. Maybe that whole thing about Mason Reed was an excuse to meet you. Even on television, before I met you, I thought you were cute. But, in person, well, you blew me away."

Jonetta was speechless, a rare condition for her. She collected her thoughts. Finally, she said, "Look, Tommy, don't get any ideas about me. I'm not easy. I'm calling you strictly as a follow-up to a story you reported. Remember?"

"Of course, I remember. But I was wrong about Reed. He's okay. A little crazy, but he's legit. I knew if I talked to you again I would have to tell you how I felt about you. The truth is, I've been dying to talk to you."

"Mason Reed aside, who are *you*, Mr. Price? I've done some checking on you and you don't seem to exist. Tommy Price. Passaic, New Jersey. Rutgers University. No such person."

Tommy couldn't believe the scope and intensity of this unexpected telephone call. Not only would he confess his love to Jonetta, but he must admit, or lie about, his true identity to the object of his affections. He sighed with resignation. "My full name is Thomas Price Friedman. Price was my mother's maiden name. She was Catholic. My dad is Jewish. Tommy Price is a stage name. You know, JJ, there are about as many Jews in country music as there are Blacks."

"Friedman?"

"Right. My father is Jacob Friedman. Friedman, Rhinehart and Bolden. Passaic, New Jersey."

"Would you spell Friedman for me?"

"F-R-I-E-D-M-A-N." He continued, "At Rutgers you can call Dr. Peter Covington. He was my senior adviser. He's in the philosophy department. I don't have his number at my fingertips, but I'll get it if you insist."

"That's not necessary."

"You see, Jonetta, I gave up a lot to come down here, carry a guitar, wear cowboy boots, and sing through my nose."

"Well, good luck, Mr. Whoever-You-Are, and goodbye." Then she hung up without waiting for his reply.

ELEVEN

The driveway to Mason Reed's mansion turned off Franklin Road about ten miles south of Nashville and snaked through a heavily wooded area, slowly ascending the side of a hill, where, in another time, confederate soldiers had maintained lookouts. A half mile down the road a huge wrought-iron gate and guardhouse appeared. Sonny Boy brought his black Mercedes to a slow halt and waited for the guard.

"May I help you, sir?"

"Yeah. Mr. and Mrs. McDaniel. We're expected."

The guard checked his clipboard and nodded. "Yes, of course, Mr. McDaniel. Let me open the gate for you. Good evening, sir. Good evening, ma'am."

Sonny Boy smiled as the gates parted. He looked at Tina, who could have stopped a parade with the outfit she was wearing. Damn, he thought, she is one fine looking female. I guess that's why I married her. Barely twenty-one, Tina was fifteen years younger than Sonny Boy, a fact he appreciated, was sensitive to, and sensitive about. He appreciated the youthful tone of her legs and the youthful firmness of her breasts. He was sensitive to her youthful need to learn and grow, so he cut her a lot of slack. But, he was sensitive *about* her age, and a sure way to raise his inbred redneck ire was to comment about the disparity in their ages.

"Oh, baby," Tina said as she put her hand on his thigh. "I think I'm gonna like Mr. Mason Reed."

"Yeah, he's one helluva guy. I thought I'd seen it all, baby, and you know ol' Sonny's seen a lot. But I never saw nothing like Mason Reed holding forth on the future of Nashville. They say the guy has a hundred and sixty I.Q."

"It seems to me Mr. Reed specializes in big numbers, like, for instance, four hundred and fifty thousand," Tina whispered, referring to the signing bonus Sonny Boy had recently deposited in a not-so-secret bank account. He had thought she didn't know about it, but she had her sources.

Sonny Boy shot a glance at Tina. The bitch knows, he realized. How in the hell did I expect to hide almost half a million dollars from her? The woman has a nose for money a bloodhound would envy. He shook his head at his foolishness for trying to deceive her.

"Look, Teenie, I'll cut you a check for ninety thou next week. You put it in your account. It's all yours, just like we agreed."

According to their prenuptial agreement, Tina was entitled to twenty percent of any payment, fee, or advance to Sonny Boy in excess of one hundred thousand dollars, so-called "extraordinary receipts." The same formula applied to Tina, but so far in their marriage, she had never received more than two hundred and twenty dollars in one payment. Sonny Boy had insisted on the prenup, but Tina, with the assistance of a shrewd New York attorney, had negotiated it to her ultimate advantage. Therefore, she was indeed entitled to ninety thousand dollars. She knew it, he knew it, and now he knew she knew.

Besides the money, there was the issue of trust. "Sonny, why didn't you just tell me about the bonus? Didn't you know I'd find out? You can't hide an elephant on a football field, sweetie. What *were* you thinking?"

"Baby, I swear I was gonna tell you. I just wanted a little

time to enjoy having it. I wasn't going to spend it. It felt good just knowing it was in the bank. Once I pay you, the bank, Mama, Uncle Sam, well, I'm not going to have much left over. Maybe a measly sixty grand. Teenie, I can burn sixty grand in a couple a months!"

"You mean to tell me, Sonny Boy, that I'll end up with more money than you? Oh my, what a strange turn of events." Tina smiled sweetly and stroked his crotch. "If you're nice to me, honey, maybe I'll give you some of mine." Then she reached over and nibbled his ear, biting him playfully.

One thing for sure, Sonny Boy thought as he felt himself become aroused, Tina is a hellcat. "Baby," he said meekly, "don't be mad at papa. I'm really sorry. Let's don't fight about money. Let's have fun tonight. Pretty soon, money will be the last of our worries."

He carefully parked the mammoth Mercedes in a lighted area. He didn't see any other cars. "Small party," he said to Tina as they climbed a lighted walkway to the house.

"Are we early?" she asked.

"Naw. In fact, we're a little late. I guess it's gonna be an intimate affair. No problem."

It was hard to tell much about the house in the dark, except that it was modern, even radical, in design. Concrete slabs and giant oak beams combined to create a remarkable effect. The house seemed to grow out of the hill. The imposing entrance was oriental in style, with an elaborate brass and ivory doorbell.

Mason answered the door with a broad grin. "Hey, Sonny! And *this . . . this* must be Tina! Sonny, you never told me you were married to a movie star. Tina, baby, come inside! Mr. McDaniel, you can go home now." With that remark, Mason grabbed Tina by the hand, pulled her inside and closed the door in Sonny Boy's face. Then, without missing a beat, the door reopened and Mason smiled. "Just kidding."

After a perfunctory tour of his eight-thousand-square-foot showplace, Mason and his guests relaxed in the sunken living room, looking out huge walls of glass at the foggy valley below. Sonny Boy broke the silence. "This must be the best view in Nashville, Mason. Spectacular. I think it beats the view from your office." Sonny Boy could lay on the charm when he wanted.

"Thank you, Sonny. I like being up high. Way up high, like an eagle scouting worlds to conquer. It inspires me."

"Mr. Reed," Tina piped up.

"Tina, *Please* call me Mason. Now, what can I do for you, my love?"

"Can you tell us the history of your home? It's just magnificent."

"Oh, yes, my dear. Thank you for asking. The house was built in 1948 by a very wealthy man named Tucker, who made a lot of money in World War II. He eventually went bankrupt, and the house has had several owners since. The most notable thing about this house is probably its architect, William Paul Manning, an important disciple of Frank Lloyd Wright. He designed the house to be an organic extension of the surrounding trees and rocks. I think he succeeded, don't you?"

Sonny Boy and Tina nodded dutifully, fully cognizant that Mason had paid over two million dollars for the house and six acres, making it one of the most expensive residences in Tennessee.

Susan Glass appeared at the top of the steps leading down into the sunken living room. She wore a gauzy white pantsuit, which revealed enough to convince Sonny Boy that she was not wearing any underclothes. Sonny Boy rose.

"Sonny Boy, sit down. Introduce me to your companion," Susan instructed him.

"Sure. Ah, Susan, this is my wife, Tina. Tina, this is Susan Glass, Mason's right hand man. Or, I should say, right hand woman."

"No, Sonny, you got it right the first time," Susan said with a smirk. "Tina, honey, you're simply gorgeous. Have you ever done any modeling?"

Tina blushed. Although she knew she was beautiful, she was unaccustomed to so much overt professional attention. Usually Sonny Boy, the star, was centerstage. She was beginning to feel like a star in her own right.

"Ms. Glass, I haven't done any modeling in a long time. Not since I left Texas. Sonny doesn't want me to work. I've had some offers, but I turned all of them down."

"Sonny Boy, you've got to share this marvelous creature with the rest of the world," Mason implored. "You can't keep her all to yourself." He ogled the cleavage Tina's low-cut top displayed.

Just as Mason was about to go too far, from Sonny Boy's perspective, in praising Tina, a truly stunning couple appeared behind Susan. The woman was the most amazing redhead Sonny Boy had ever seen, and he considered himself a connoisseur of redheads. Like Susan, she was wearing a sheer pajama-like outfit. Pale peach and silky, it clung to her body. The male beside her appeared Latino, with a blinding smile and a perfect physique.

"Sonny and Tina, these are our houseguests—Margo St. John, one of my clients, and her special friend, Ernesto. They flew in from the Coast to spend the weekend with us."

After pleasantries, trivialities, and cocktails, Mason produced a perfectly rolled joint. The couples were seated, shoeless, on a large circular velvet couch, eying each other warily.

"*Voila!* This is some dynamite Hawaiian weed. Everybody try it." The joint made its way around the circle. Everyone but Tina smoked.

"Tina. What's wrong, sweetheart? Don't you like grass?" Mason asked with genuine concern.

"Oh, it's okay, I guess. But it usually gives me a headache."

"I don't think this grass will give you a headache. At seven hundred an ounce, it better not!"

"That's okay, really. I better pass."

Mason rose ceremoniously and retrieved a black lacquered box from a side table. "I have just the thing for you, luv." From the box he produced a mirror, a razor, and about a gram of cocaine. Tina's eyes lit up.

"Now that's more like it... Mason," she said and winked at her host.

"Thank you, Tina. Now we're friends." Mason prepared four generous lines of cocaine, two of which he gave to Tina, two of which he inhaled through a tightly rolled one hundred dollar bill which he kept in the black box.

"Anybody else? There's plenty where this came from."

Margo and Ernesto partook, but Sonny Boy and Susan declined. "I'll stick with the weed," Sonny Boy said. "Me and coke don't mix." This will be a long night, Sonny Boy thought, as he felt familiar, powerful cravings eroding his self-control.

Dinner was prepared and served by a middle-aged Vietnamese couple Mason had brought with him from Los Angeles. The food was exquisite, a sublime blend of French and Asian cuisines. The wines were irresistible. Every hour or so another perfect joint would materialize and make its way around the table. A couple of times, Mason and Tina excused themselves and snorted more cocaine. By dessert, flaming bananas Foster, Mason's guests were stuffed, stoned, and satiated, almost giddy from pleasure. Mason and Sonny traded show business jokes and anecdotes and kept everyone howling. Margo and Ernesto didn't say much but they smiled a lot and looked great. Susan enjoyed herself, but not too much. Tina, however, was incoherent from a nearly lethal combination of alcohol and cocaine.

Mason stood up. "Come on, people! Back to the living room, it's showtime." He walked over to the wall and pressed a series of buttons. The room darkened and a movie screen descended in front of the picture windows.

When everyone was settled, Mason announced with fanfare, "Tonight we have a special treat, a new film featuring our very own... Margo and Ernesto!"

Tina perked up and mumbled, "Margo and Ernesto? Are y'all in your own movie? That's neat! Whazit called?"

Margo answered grandly, "The working title is *Passion Fruit*. It has a travel motif. We shot it in Bali last month. I think it's my best work. And Ernesto is fabulous."

Passion Fruit began rolling, beamed from an overhead projector behind the couples. As they sank into the couches, Mason dimmed the lights further. Within minutes, the screen was filled with explicit images of Margo and Ernesto making savage love on a beach at sunset. The sexual tension in the room built to the exploding point. Slowly, Margo rose in front of the screen and began a provocative striptease. At the crowd's urging, Susan joined her. As they removed each other's clothing, they kissed and caressed each other. When they were both nude, they coaxed Tina into joining them. As she began removing her clothes, Mason turned off the film's audio, left it running, and filled the room with seductive rhythm and blues from his state-of-the-art sound system. Tina stole the show, demonstrating a sensuality so fervent it frightened Sonny Boy.

The party lasted until dawn, fueled by a high octane mix of sex, drugs, and rock 'n roll. When it was over Mason, Susan, Sonny Boy, Tina, Margo, and Ernesto had all become very close.

TWELVE

By the early summer of 1992, within months of his arrival, Mason was ahead of schedule with his Nashville strategy. The city had welcomed him with open arms, and he had quickly established himself as a major player. Eagle Records, his new label, had signed half a dozen artists, including Sonny Boy, whom American Records had released for a token one thousand dollars. Eagle had signed a distribution deal with Polygram, the Dutch giant, and was preparing its first radio and video releases. Sonny Boy had met his negotiated weight loss goal and was feeling like a new man, convinced his first number one record was only months away. Tommy was winning Mason over to the value of music publishing, and Mason was increasingly impressed with the young man's potential as an executive. He told Tommy, "You think like a Jew," which was about the highest compliment Mason could give someone.

It especially pleased Mason that Susan had finally adapted to Nashville. Initially, she had fought their relocation from the Coast. Without Susan, Mason knew he would be lost. They had been together more than nine years, an unusual but effective couple. When they met he was a rising star at the William Morris Agency and she was a struggling actress and very high-priced hooker. He had frequently employed her services as a prostitute, not for himself, but for his clients. He had even managed to secure for her a few acting jobs in low-budget thrillers and bimbo pictures. Against all odds, they had become the closest of friends. Indeed, Susan was Mason's only friend, and vice versa.

Despite, or maybe because of, his homosexuality, Mason had always liked prostitutes. He was fascinated by their take on life, love, money, and sex. To his way of thinking, everyone was a whore to some degree. At least hookers were honest about selling out.

By the time Susan tired of the flesh trade, Mason had his own agency, and he hired her as his personal assistant. As he had intuited, she quickly proved a natural. Now, when he needed the services of a high class hooker, he called Margo St. John, who was a legendary sexual animal. Already, Margo had proved very helpful in Nashville. The secret sex videotapes he had made of Margo and Sonny Boy could provide Mason valuable leverage in future contract negotiations with McDaniel.

In addition to his successful moves on Music Row, Mason invested in other businesses as well. He bought real estate, stocks, bonds, certificates of deposit, mortgages, almost anything reasonable that crossed his desk. He was under considerable pressure from his partner to find safe havens for ever increasing sums of money. Christ, Mason never knew there was so much money in the world! Last month, he had purchased the Crown Tower, where his offices were located, and the eleventh floor was now occupied by professional money managers, accountants, and financial advisers who had little involvement with the entertainment business. In fact, the truth was, if Reed never made a dime in music or movies his partner wouldn't mind. These high profile *show* businesses drew attention away from other, more lucrative enterprises, all funded by a cascading stream of cash which flowed from banks in the Caymans, Switzerland and Hong Kong. In payment for his efforts Mason deposited a million dollars a month in his personal account.

To celebrate his good fortune and to stoke the public relations engine, Mason hosted a bus caravan from Nashville to Talladega, Alabama, where *The Richard Petty Story* was being filmed, starring Burt Reynolds in a comeback role. Mason invited his staff, his recording artists, and carefully selected members of the media for a three day party and schmooze fest. The first night in Alabama, he rented an entire bowling alley. Burt was kind enough to drop by, knock down a few pins, pose for pictures, and sign autographs. Against his better judgment, Mason had acquiesced to an on-camera interview with Jonetta Jordan from Channel Six, whom Tommy had persuaded to come along, despite her misgivings. Sonny Boy brought Tina, his mother, and Mavis, and they had a blast. Ruby graciously sang several of her signature songs at the farewell party Mason had thrown at a country dance club. Tina was thrilled at the small role Mason had arranged for her in the film. She even had a line of dialogue. All in all, it was a great trip. On the way home, they sang Beatles' songs on the bus, and everyone agreed that Mason Reed and Associates was like a big, happy family.

THIRTEEN

From the back seat of his Lincoln Continental limousine, through tinted, bullet-proof glass, Hector Armadas watched a group of boys, barely school age, steal fruit from an outdoor stand as the owner ran out and chased them with a broom. Hector smiled at his inner identification with the young-sters. Many years ago, he too had been a hungry street urchin. In a few years, he speculated, these boys might be re-cruited by his agents to attend the training school for *sicarios* he operated at his vast estate north of Medillin, La Pon-derosa.

Medellin supported several thousand *sicarios*, hired killers who worked for as little as ten dollars a hit. The *sicarios* provided simple and economical resolutions to many of life's unfortunate situations: business deals gone sour, lovers' quarrels, honest politicians. The *sicarios* and their bosses were the defacto rulers of Medellin, an outwardly progres-sive, prosperous city of over two million fearful souls.

Next to him sat his younger brother, Carlos. The two of them were orphaned when Carlos was seven, their parents having died within weeks of each other in a flu epidemic which had swept the barrio, somehow sparing the boys. Hec-tor had done his best raising Carlos, but resources and pros-pects were limited for two orphans from a poor family. Now, despite the odds against them, they were two of the richest, most powerful men in the Western Hemisphere.

"Carlos." Hector addressed his brother without looking at him.

"Sí?"

"Did you remember to wear your vest?"

"No. Screw it. It's too damn uncomfortable. When your number comes up, there's nothing you can do."

Hector shook his head at his brother's foolish fatalism and wondered if he would outlive his not-so-careful sibling. Perhaps, but not likely. In terms of life expectancy, Carlos had the great advantage of relative anonymity. In contrast, Hector's name was legend. He adjusted the strap of his own bulletproof vest and said three silent Hail Marys.

The limo pulled up at a Catholic hospital for the poor, where, today, he would cut the ceremonial ribbon and dedicate the new wing he had established for the treatment of tuberculosis. The wing was named in honor of his mother, whose portrait would hang in the lobby. That is, if the artist ever completed the painting! He didn't fault the artist. It was difficult to paint the portrait of a deceased person without the assistance of a photograph, aided only by the memory of her sons, who could hardly remember her. He and Carlos had already rejected several versions. But, in these matters, Hector was a patient man.

A dozen or so priests, doctors, and politicians were waiting for him on the hospital steps, all wearing broad smiles. He was pleased to see the archbishop in attendance. If you give more than a million dollars, Hector mused, you get the archbishop. He and the archbishop had been congenial for many years, and they both savored the warm understanding which flows between powerful men.

Before he exited the car, two bodyguards jumped out, armed with Uzi submachine guns, and surveyed the crowd. After they signaled all clear, Hector opened his door. For all his wealth and power, he was not a free man. When he was a starving street punk, he was free. Now he was the well-fed, pampered prisoner of his own fame and fortune. Life is paradox, he thought.

The archbishop embraced him in a heartfelt bear hug. "Don Hector, we thought you might not make it."

"Forgive me, Padre, for being tardy. The traffic."

"Yes, of course, my son. But you're here now and we are so honored. Have you seen the beautiful new wing your generous gift made possible?"

"No, Padre. Unfortunately, I rarely leave La Ponderosa. But my people have kept me informed."

"Yes, my son. Let us proceed inside. The staff and patients have prepared a welcoming ceremony for you, complete with cake and lemonade."

A photographer snapped an informal picture of the assembled dignitaries, but one of Hector's bodyguards quickly confiscated the camera, knocking down the photographer in the process. Hector looked sheepishly at the archbishop.

"I'm sorry, Padre, but my men are trained to prevent me from being photographed. I prefer to perform my charitable work anonymously. If you don't mind?"

"Of course, my son. I understand. Our Savior taught us that when we give, our left hand should not know what our right hand is doing." The archbishop held his palms up and then turned his left hand down. Hector smiled. The group entered the hospital as the frightened photographer got up, dusted himself off, and retrieved his empty camera from the unsmiling bodyguard.

◆

As the day ended at La Ponderosa, Hector was in a serene mood, reflecting on the events at the hospital. His English butler served high tea to him and his wife, Elena, complete with crumpets, scones, and marmalade. The couple was silent as they sat on the veranda overlooking several acres of manicured gardens, fountains, and statuary. A pleasant late afternoon breeze stirred the fresh cut flowers on the table. Hector added milk and sugar to his tea and stirred it slowly. A morning cup of coffee and afternoon tea were the strongest drink or drugs he ingested.

"How did it go today in the city?" Elena asked softly.

"Very nicely. The archbishop was there, and also Senator Ruiz. The children at the hospital performed a song they had written for the occasion. It was very touching."

The couple lapsed into a comfortable silence as Elena buttered a crumpet for him. She was a handsome woman with the regal bearing of Spanish aristocracy. Her father, Domingo Manuel de Silva, was an important Medillin cattle baron, though of late, Don Manuel had fallen on hard times. Last year, Hector gladly gave the old man seven hundred thousand dollars to save his ranch. Hector's gift represented a symbolic turning of the tables. Twenty years before, when he had asked Don Manuel for Elena's hand in marriage, her father had spat in his face. Elena and Hector had eloped, and for years her parents would not speak to them. Slowly, they came around, as Hector's fortune and influence increased to international proportions. Her mother, in fact, spent most of her time at La Ponderosa, unable to resist the attraction of her grandchildren.

Elena was Hector's first and only wife, and would remain so, until death. He did not believe in nor condone divorce. He did, however, maintain several mistresses in the city. His visits to them, including today's after the dedication, were among the rare trips he made into Medillin. Elena knew about Hector's women, but what could she do? As much as Hector, she was also a prisoner of his wealth and notoriety.

But she accepted her situation with grace and proceeded with steely resolve to provide her family with as normal a life as possible, given their unique circumstances.

"Elena."

"Yes, my dear?"

"I have invited some American business associates to spend a week with us next month. I expect we'll have four or five guests. I want to provide them the very best hospitality La Ponderosa has to offer. This is important to me. Will you see to it that all the necessary arrangements are made?"

"Of course, Hector. I enjoy visitors, especially Americans. I can practice my English. May I ask the nature of your dealings with them?"

Hector frowned at her question but responded anyway. "Entertainment. Music. Movies. To be more specific, country music."

"Wonderful! How exciting." Elena shared her husband's enthusiasm for country music, having acquired her taste for it from him.

Hector smiled and motioned for the butler to replenish his tea cup. Seven white egrets landed on the lake below and Hector took it as a good omen.

FOURTEEN

Gus Rogers lived in a converted attic apartment on Nineteenth Avenue, only four blocks from the company offices at Crown Tower. A rusty set of metal steps led up to a side entrance. On the door, a hand painted sign read, "PNR Enterprises."

As unlikely as it seemed, Tommy considered Gus, a fifty-seven-year-old recovering alcoholic from the Kentucky hills, to be his best friend. They had met about three years ago when Gus had approached Tommy after an open mic night at the Bluebird Cafe. That night, Tommy had performed two originals. Gus had said to Tommy, "Hey, kid. You're good. And, remember, it takes one to know one."

A great friendship was born that night. After the show, Tommy followed Gus back to this same attic apartment, and they shared songs and a bottle of Jim Beam until the mockingbirds heralded dawn. They reconvened a few nights later, and Gus eventually listened to every song Tommy had ever written, at least four dozen. Gus then informed Tommy that he had heard "two or three good 'uns."

On the other hand, Gus awed Tommy with one great song after another, each perfectly crafted and polished by years of "fiddlin'," each built around a kernel of truth. Even more amazing to Tommy was the fact that Gus had received almost no recognition and precious little reward for his immense talent and perseverance. He didn't consider that fact hopeful regarding his own prospects. But, Gus reassured him that if he would "learn from my screw-ups," Tommy could succeed. In Tommy's eyes, Gus was like the Van Gogh of Music Row, a tragic but compelling figure, unlike anyone he had ever known.

In the same room where they had sat that first night trading songs, Gus watched Tommy re-string an acoustic Gibson guitar. This time, there was no bottle. Last year, Gus had quit drinking and joined a twelve-step program. Out of deference and in support of his sobriety, Tommy didn't drink around him. Tommy wound the high E string and then clipped the excess with a wire cutter.

"Hey, gimme an E," Tommy said.

Gus picked up his ancient Martin and plucked the high string. Within a few minutes, they were in tune, a condition Gus absolutely required for music making. For Gus, being in tune carried mystical implications. Singers and pickers who played out of tune were dismissed by Gus as poseurs, fakes, wannabes.

"Man, it's been so long since I played, I've lost my callouses. It hurts." Tommy moaned as he rubbed his sore fingertips.

"Yeah, kid, you're so busy being a big shot executive you keep forgetting why you came here. To write!"

"Somebody has to make something happen. Don't bitch. Tonight, you're getting a cut thanks to me."

Gus smiled at the prospect of Sonny Boy McDaniel recording his song, "Wayward Angel." Talk was, if it came off well in the studio, "Wayward Angel" would be a single. A hit single in today's market meant big money for the songwriter, maybe six figures. Gus put his forefinger to his lips and whispered, "Shhhh. Don't jinx it. It ain't final 'til it's vinyl. At least that's what we used to say, when they put records out on wax."

"Trust me. It's in the bag. We *know* it's a great song. Let's

65

just hope Sonny Boy nails it. Say, how long has it been since you got a cut?"

Gus rubbed his chin and reflected. "Damn. Over nine years. Thumper Tate. But he never finished it. Too drunk. That was back in one of his bad spells."

"That must've been hard on you, getting so close to a record by the world's greatest country singer, and then missing it."

"Yeah. It was hard. I figured if Thumper took drunk, I would, too. And I did, for about three years. Like I keep telling you, you could learn a lot from my mistakes."

"Gus."

"Yeah, kid?"

"What's your take on Mason? Have you seen anything suspicious? You're with him so much, I thought maybe you had picked up on something."

"Nope. Nothing yet. But, man, he *is* an operator. Whenever he's with me, that carphone is in his ear and he's barking at it. Now and then, I'll see him in the rear view mirror snorting up. And, he's definitely a three dollar bill. I reckon I've carried at least a dozen young men out to his place. But, so far, no sign of Hector ah..."

"Armadas."

"Yeah, Armadas. Course, don't you figure he'd be pretty careful about something like that? I mean I can't prove he's *not* in business with South American funny money. When it comes to people..."

"I know. Nothing surprises you. I heard yesterday that Mason and Sonny Boy are going to the Caribbean after the sessions. I think that's a little weird. Maybe they're sweet for each other."

"No way. Sonny Boy's a straight arrow in that department. Anyway, what's wrong with a little R and R? They got money to burn."

"It's the timing. For them to be gone over a week when we've got so much to do to get this record out... I dunno. It's strange, that's all."

"Yeah, sure. I agree they're strange. But everybody in this town is a little strange. Speaking of strange. Still have the hots for that black girl? Have you told your old man about her?"

"She got engaged last week. To a lawyer. And no, I never told my dad. He wouldn't dig it. But, I still think about her. A lot. Someday, I'll write a song about the whole experience."

"Yeah, if you don't quit writing." Gus began strumming a D chord and Tommy joined in. They played until Gus' beeper went off, signifying his summons by Mason.

◆

Later that night from somewhere in the nothingness of a deep sleep cycle, Tommy slowly awakened to the gentle ringing of his bedside phone, which was set on the lowest decibel. He rolled across the bed and checked the luminous digital clock as he reached for the receiver. 2:12 A.M. 'Who in the hell?' he thought.

"Hullo," he said wearily.

"Price. Get up! Christ, are you in a coma? I let it ring a dozen times."

Tommy recognized the staccato voice of his master. "Mr. Reed. Yes sir. How can I help you?" Tommy asked.

"Get dressed. We'll pick you up in fifteen minutes. They're putting down the final vocals on Sonny Boy at the Song Factory. Gus and I thought you'd like to check it out."

"Right. Yes sir. I'll be ready."

He waited dutifully at the bottom of the driveway which

led to the guest house he rented from Mrs. Wallace. He pulled his jacket over his head to protect himself from a cool, steady mist. He saw the limo approach. When it stopped, he jumped in the front seat with Gus.

From the back, Mason said, "What's the matter, kid? Are you scared of me? Come back here. I want to talk to you."

Tommy and Gus exchanged a shrug and Tommy got out, ran around the car, entered the passenger compartment and sat across from Mason, who looked wide awake but bored. Bobby, the bodyguard, was asleep in the other corner.

"Yes sir, Mr. Reed. Thanks for calling. That was very thoughtful. I hope things are going well at the studio..."

"Oh, shut up, Price. Don't patronize me. It's two-thirty in the morning. You're probably pissed at me for waking you up."

Tommy shook his head. "No, no, really, I'm glad to be here. I'm excited about this project. Hey, Mr. Reed," he grinned gamely, "show business is my life."

Mason was silent as they drove to the Song Factory, one of Nashville's premier recording studios. The Song Factory was a recent addition to the city's expanding list of world-class studios, offering the finest in digital recording and computer assisted mixing capabilities. At three hundred an hour, only the best budgeted artists could work there.

Finally, Reed spoke. "Price, I'm impressed with your work in the publishing game. I understand we own eight of the songs Sonny Boy has recorded. That's good. I'm beginning to see how those publishing pennies could add up."

Eager for a pat on the back, Tommy relished Mason's praise. He had worked hard to place House of Reed songs on the McDaniel sessions. He and Kraselsky had screened over a thousand songs. In the process, he had developed a rapport with Sonny Boy's record producer, Adam Speer, a twenty-something wunderkind Mason had imported from the Coast.

"Thank you, sir. We did find some great material. Adam has a good ear. I just hope Sonny Boy can hook the vocals."

"Don't worry about McDaniel. Adam will make him deliver. If not, I'll kill both of them!" Mason had a way of slightly unnerving Tommy.

The entrance to the Song Factory was locked and monitored by a video scanner. After identifying themselves through a speaker phone, the door clicked and they entered. Immediately, Tommy smelled money. The studio was decorated in the Santa Fe style, with western art, pink Mexican tile and tan leather furniture. The walls were lined with framed platinum albums which had been recorded there. The Factory had hosted some of the hottest names in country music. Tommy discreetly tallied the artists represented on the walls as he walked the long hallway to the control room. By now, Tommy was wide awake. He looked at Gus and smiled. To his surprise, Gus seemed nervous and agitated. Then he realized why. "Wayward Angel." Would Gus' nine year drought end tonight?

The Song Factory actually consisted of three separate studios. Adam and Sonny Boy were in studio A. Mason and his entourage quietly entered the rear of the control room, which was almost dark, lit only by the soft glow from the control panels. At the board two figures sat in swivel chairs. In the main room, on the other side of the glass, Sonny Boy stood in his sock feet, wearing earphones, facing a microphone and a music stand with a light.

Adam Speer swung his chair around. He was chubby with a long ponytail and wore wire-rimmed glasses.

"Mason! Come on in. What are you doing up at this hour? Meet Ron Vincent, my engineer. Ron, this is the infamous Mason Reed, our employer. I flew Ron in from L.A. in an effort to save the project. Mason, you didn't tell me this doofus is incapable of singing in tune."

Gus winced. Tommy shifted his weight nervously.

"But," Adam continued, "I *think* we can use Ron's magic pitch bender to get Sonny Boy right on the note. Nobody will ever know! Thank God for computers."

The group relaxed collectively. A lot was at stake. "Good, Adam, good! That's what I pay you for. Make it sound good, or else!" Mason released one of his inimitable cackles.

When they had entered the control room, Tommy had spotted the barefoot redhead curled on a couch, reading a *Cosmopolitan* magazine with a pocket flashlight. Now, she got up, stretched feline-like and headed for Mason.

"Sweetie-pie, are you ready for our little trip?" she asked Mason as she patted his bald spot and pecked his cheek.

"Margo, baby, I can't wait! Are you enjoying the recording studio? Have you learned anything from these highly paid experts?"

"Yeah, I've learned that making records is just as boring as making movies." She turned her attention to Tommy. "And who is this fine specimen?"

"Margo, meet Thomas Price, the head of my music publishing companies. But you better keep your paws off him. I think Susan has already claimed him for herself."

Margo moved toward Tommy, undeterred. "Well, hello, Mr. Price. Are you going to Barbados with us? I hope so. I'd like to learn more about publishing. I've written a song or two myself. I think they're hits. Would you let me sing them for you?"

Tommy coughed. "Why, of course. But I'm not going to Barbados. Maybe we can talk when you get back."

Suddenly, a voice boomed over the speakers. "What the hell is going on in there? Christ, Adam, it'll be dawn before we finish!" An impatient Sonny Boy was unaware that Mason had arrived.

"Sorry, Sonny. The boss is here," Adam said into the talkback.

Sonny Boy's tone changed instantly. "Oh, I see. Mason, my main man! Have a seat. We're working on 'Wayward Angel.' It sounds great... I think."

The engineer pushed a button and the tracks rolled as Sonny Boy picked up where he had stopped.

Wayward Angel
Where have you gone?
You left me in a living hell
All alone, all alone

Adam stopped the song. "Sonny, try it again. You're still flat in a couple of spots." The tape rolled again.

Wayward Angel
Where have you gone?
You left me in a living hell
All alone, all alone

Adam turned to his visitors. "See what I mean. The cat *cannot* stay on the note. He's all around it. Over. Under. And this is such a great song. It's a crime against music to waste it."

Tommy couldn't let the moment pass. He spoke up. "I'd like everyone to know the writer of this great song is standing over there, Gus Rogers."

Adam swiveled toward Gus. "Great song, man. Don't worry, Ron and I will fix it in the mix. I promise."

After more prodding from Adam and with chemical assistance from Mason, Sonny Boy finally finished his vocals a little after four A.M. When Adam excused him, Sonny Boy let out a whoop, "Barbados, here I come!"

FIFTEEN

The Gulfstream was fueled and waiting at Lemley Field, a private airport forty miles southeast of Nashville. Gus pulled up about fifty yards from the plane and jumped out to assist his passengers: Mason, Sonny Boy, Margo, Ernesto, and Bobby. They emerged from the limo in various states of inebriation, the party having started an hour earlier. Sonny Boy was draped over Margo, who was wearing a bikini top and wrap-around skirt, still sleepy from the studio marathon the night before. Ernesto had gotten a full night's sleep and looked like he was headed for a fashion shoot. He stayed close to Mason, who, as always, issued orders to anyone and everyone crossing his path. Bobby, the bodyguard, wore sunglasses and baggy Bermuda shorts. In six months, Gus had never heard Bobby speak. Gus assumed he was mute.

Gus and Bobby hauled the luggage from the limo to the plane. The sun was setting, but the black, sticky asphalt runway emitted wave after wave of Tennessee summer heat, providing further incentive for a quick departure.

After completing his baggage duties, Gus moseyed over to chat with Jimmy, Mason's chief pilot. Gus had always been fascinated by planes, and he harbored a private ambition to earn his pilot's license.

"Beautiful bird," Gus said as he ran his hand over the plane's glossy white surface.

"Yeah, top of the line," Jimmy replied as he made notations on a clip board.

"Say, Jimmy, what does a plane like this cost? If you don't mind me asking?"

"'Bout ten million plus change. This baby belonged to Kenny Rogers."

"My, my. Ten million dollars. Say, Jimmy, I hear you're headed to Barbados."

Jimmy looked up and said, "Yeah, Barbados and ... points south." Then he pushed up his sunglasses and winked at Gus.

Gus nodded but said nothing. Jimmy tore off a sheet of paper. "Hey, Gus, do me a favor and turn this in at the control tower. That would save me a little time. This crowd is raring to go."

"Sure, Jimmy. Be glad to." Gus took the folded paper. "Have a good flight. I'll be waiting when you get back."

Jimmy saluted Gus, and within minutes Gus was watching the jet's blinking lights disappear into the dark eastern sky.

◆

On the way back to Nashville, Gus picked up the car-phone and called Tommy, who was still at work.

"Tommy, this is Gus."

"Hey, man! Guess what! You have the first single on Sonny Boy McDaniel. It's official. I just talked to Adam and 'Wayward Angel' is it! Let me be the first to congratulate you. Your losing streak has ended, partner. How does it feel?"

"Great. It feels great," Gus said distractedly.

"What's wrong? I thought you'd be excited. Adam says the record is a smash. They processed the vocal through a computer. Everything's in tune. And Mason approved a video budget this morning before he left. So, what's the problem?"

"Look, kid, I'm real happy about the song. Thanks for all your help, but I need to talk to you. Soon. So meet me at Mac's Diner in about twenty minutes. It's important."

◆

Tommy was finishing a cup of coffee and a cigarette when Gus walked into Mac's wearing his chauffeur's uniform. Gus motioned to the waitress for coffee, looked Tommy in the eye and got right to the point.

"Kid, we got a problem. A big problem."

Tommy lit another smoke. "I'm listening."

"I just got back from Lemley Field, where I deposited Mason and Sonny Boy and other assorted freaks."

"Right. Barbados. R and R."

"When I mentioned Barbados to Jimmy, the pilot, he winked at me and added 'points south' as their destination."

"Points south?"

"Yeah. Then he gave me the flight plan and asked me to file it. Before I did, I glanced at it. Final destination . . . Medillin, Colombia. Looks like all your suspicions have been confirmed. And I thought you were being paranoid. Well, I was wrong and you were right."

They both sipped their coffees, Gus wishing it were something stronger. Gus bummed a smoke from Tommy. His hands shook slightly as he lit it. Tommy gazed blankly out the window as night descended.

Tommy brightened. "Maybe it's a joke. Why would they file a flight plan like that? The feds would jump on it. Medillin? That's a red flag for the DEA. Too risky. It doesn't add up."

"Sure it adds up. Like two plus two. Don't you know that Reed *bought* Lemley Field? That's right. He owns the airplane and the airport. Very convenient. The feds will never see that flight plan. Lemley is probably where the cocaine comes in. Jimmy and all the rest of 'em are in on it. I'd bet my Martin guitar they're gonna pay a visit to a certain Señor Ar... ah... Ar..."

"Armadas, Gus. Hector Armadas." Tommy spoke the name softly.

SIXTEEN

The next morning in Barbados, Mason woke up in bed with Ernesto and, across the hall, Sonny Boy snored beside Margo. In the hallway between the suites Bobby manned his post, straining a folding chair with his bulk, reading a comic book. Mason checked his watch. Ten A.M., Nashville time. He called Sonny Boy's room.

Margo answered, "Yeah. Who is it?"

"Margo, baby, it's Mason. Rise and shine. Lemme talk to lover boy."

"Sure. Anything to stop him snoring. Jesus, no wonder he's been through three wives. He's a friggin' freight train."

Sonny Boy took the receiver. "Mason, for God's sake. This is *my* vacation, remember?"

"I need to talk to you, Sonny. Meet me in the restaurant in thirty minutes."

"Can it wait?"

"No, it can't."

"Okay, hoss. I'll be there in an hour."

"Thirty minutes, I said."

"Forty-five. I'll be there in forty-five."

◆

Mason was attacking a pair of eggs Benedict when Sonny Boy entered the restaurant. Once again, Mason's stamina amazed him. After a hard plane trip and an all night party, there he sits fresh as a garden rose. The man ain't human,

Sonny Boy thought. He joined Mason and ordered a Bloody Mary.

"Hair of the dog?" Mason asked.

"Yeah. I can't even remember last night but I think I had fun. Now I hurt like hell."

"Was Margo good to you?"

"Incredible. That wench could suck Canada dry. Look, if Tina ever finds out..."

Mason made the motion of zipping his mouth, then changed the subject. "Sonny, I know I told you we would be here a week, but our plans have changed. We're leaving this afternoon."

"What? Leaving Barbados? What in the hell for? Is something wrong back home?"

"No, no. Everything is right, real right. Perfect, in fact."

"So, what gives?"

"I told you I have a silent partner. Well, lucky you, he's a big fan of yours, and really wants to meet you. Truth is, he insists. And this is the best time to do it."

"*This* is the best time to do it? My vacation? Fuck him."

"No, Sonny. Don't talk that way. This is serious, or I wouldn't bring it up."

Sonny Boy sighed as he considered the situation. Mason was good, the best, but his demands were sometimes unreasonable. "Okay, let's fly him to Barbados. He can join the fun," Sonny Boy suggested hopefully.

"That's not possible, Sonny. We have to go see him. But, he's got a great place with lots to do. Golf, horses, hunting, fishing, everything. You'll have a good time. I guarantee it."

The waiter brought his drink and Sonny Boy drained half the glass. When the waiter asked what he would like for breakfast, Sonny Boy ordered another Bloody Mary and coffee.

"Mason, I don't like sudden changes in plans. It throws me off balance. Tina thinks we're down here for a week, sequencing the album. Now what'll I tell her?"

"Don't worry, I'll handle Tina. I'll call her after breakfast." Sonny Boy didn't know that Tina and Jerry Suddath were house-sitting Mason's mansion. Mason sipped the freshly squeezed orange juice and smiled at Sonny Boy, waiting for the next move in their verbal sparring.

"Okay, so where are we going to meet Mr. X? And, by the way, who is this guy?" Sonny Boy asked.

"This *guy* is my partner. That should say it all. You'll know who he is soon enough. Just be ready to leave at three. That'll give you time to hit the beach. But, we're leaving at three o'clock. Sharp!"

Sonny Boy didn't like this turn of events. He was desperate for a rest. Making the album had stretched him to the breaking point. Adam Speer was a genius but a prick, a perfectionist without mercy. Sonny Boy knew he had done his best studio work ever, but he was exhausted. Now, it looked like more work. Mason had told him almost nothing about his mysterious silent partner, except that he was fantastically wealthy, a stickler for privacy, and a country music fanatic. Sonny Boy wasn't too troubled by the secrecy surrounding Mason's source of funding; he understood that rich people were circumspect in their dealings. To a degree, Sonny Boy was rich himself, and he wanted to be a lot richer. He liked rich people, liked being around them. Now, at least, he would learn the identity of the man behind Mason.

Mason reached across the table and patted his arm. "Trust me, Sonny, I'm your manager. If you can't trust me, who can you trust? What's good for you is good for me and vice versa. Things are going great. You just made a great record, your best ever. My partner wants to shake your hand

and hear the rough mixes. He's even got some ideas on future songs. Hey, this guy is gonna invest a ton of money in your career. Whatever it takes to put you on top! He's a fascinating guy. You'll like him. It won't be like work at all. You'll have Margo to keep you company. And, if you like, my partner, hey, buddy, *our* partner can arrange for you to meet some other ladies. It'll be fun. Trust me."

Sonny Boy had counted on the red-headed exhibitionist entertaining him for the next few days. But, by mid-week, he might enjoy some sexual variety. From what he knew of Margo, she might, too. He decided to play the good sport. No problem.

"Mason, you beat all. You're full of surprises. I guess that's your style. Just keep Tina in the dark and off my back and I'm all yours. Let's go see Daddy Warbucks. I'm always interested in meeting my fans, especially millionaires."

"Correction, my friend. Billionaire. A mul-tee-billion-aire"

"Damn, I never met a billionaire. Might be enlightening."

◆

The jet left the island of Barbados and turned on a south-westerly course. Before long, the blue green Atlantic disappeared, and they were flying over dense vegetation, rivers and lakes. After an hour or so, Sonny Boy asked the pilot, "How far is it?" Jimmy did not reply. Everyone smiled at Sonny Boy. Behind him, Bobby prepared a syringe. Margo was whispering in Sonny Boy's ear when Bobby grabbed his shoulder. He felt a sharp pain in the back of his arm, like a bad bee sting. Margo caught him around the neck and kissed him hard on the mouth. He felt hot liquid enter his arm. Within seconds, he was spinning. A minute later, he was unconscious.

As Mason watched his star go limp, he kicked his brief-case in anger. He couldn't believe he had acquiesced to Hector's insane demands to bring Sonny Boy to Medillin. The risks were enormous. But Hector was unrelenting, threatening to scuttle the entire deal unless Mason agreed. Mason shook his head as he gazed down at the green hills of South America. Damn, this is stupid. Stupid and risky. To Mason, stupidity was inexcusable, in himself and in others.

◆

Many hours later, Sonny Boy became vaguely aware of a sound. He opened one eye and attempted to locate the steady knocking noise. He spotted a big grandfather clock as the source. It appeared out of focus, but he thought it read ten after seven. He didn't know if it was day or night. His head ached with a dull throbbing. His right arm was sore. His mouth was very dry and he became conscious of a strong thirst. On the bedside table he saw a large crystal pitcher filled with ice water, perspiring from condensation. Beside it, a crystal tumbler. He drank two glasses, then fell back in bed and slept another ten hours.

The next time he awoke, he felt a hand on his shoulder. He heard a voice calling his name. It was Margo.

"Sonny Boy. Sonny, wake up. Wake up, sweetie. You gotta get up. Are you all right?"

Sonny Boy looked unknowingly at the pretty woman hovering above him like an apparition. "Who are you? And where in the hell am I?" he mumbled to her.

Margo looked hurt. "Sonny, don't you remember me? I'm Margo. Margo. Remember?"

Sonny Boy searched his befuddled mind. Margo, Tina, Teresa, Jane, Sherry, Debbie, Lisa. Their faces came in and out of focus in his memory.

"Where's my mama? I want my mama," he said with childlike panic.

Another face appeared. Mason. "Your mama's back in Nashville. Listen, Sonny Boy, it's time to get up. You've got a show in three hours." Sonny Boy began drifting away again. Mason picked up the water pitcher and dumped its icy contents on Sonny Boy's head. Sonny Boy gasped.

"I said, get up! It's showtime. Now get the hell out of bed."

"A show? Where am I? Where's Ruby? Mavis?"

Mason looked at Margo and shook his head in disgust at his pathetic client. He hated this situation. Hated it! Obviously, Bobby had overdosed Sonny Boy. Lucky we didn't kill him, Mason thought. The important thing was to rally him for his command performance. Hector had invited over two hundred prominent Colombians to be entertained by Sonny Boy McDaniel, the famous American country music star. Mason was frantic.

"Go get some coffee. The stronger, the better," he commanded Margo. She left the room.

"Listen to me, Sonny Boy. You got sick on the plane, but you're okay now. You've got a show in three hours. A big show. Maybe the most important show of you life. So get the hell up! Both of our butts are on the line."

Sonny Boy rolled over, fell out of bed, and moaned.

SEVENTEEN

Ten years before, on his last trip to the United States, Hector visited a huge record store in Houston, Texas, called the Purple Armadillo. The Purple Armadillo claimed to offer the world's largest selection of country music, Hector's favorite. He bought everything he didn't have by Merle Haggard, Johnny Cash, Waylon Jennings, Willie Nelson, Marty Robbins, and, on a hunch, an album by a singer he didn't know, Sonny Boy McDaniel. He liked the album cover. It showed Sonny Boy dressed like a gunfighter, standing on a dusty street, aiming two colt revolvers at the reader. The album was titled <u>Buy This Record or I'll Shoot You</u>. Hector liked that. *Macho.*

Back home, after repeated listenings, Hector discovered several great songs on Sonny Boy's album. He liked Sonny Boy's vocal style and the band was first rate, some of Nashville's finest pickers. Hector subscribed to *Billboard* magazine, and he followed the album's progress with interest. He watched as four successive singles from the record made their way up the charts, only to stall before reaching the top forty. In his opinion, American Records had chosen the wrong songs to highlight as singles. He believed he possessed an uncanny knack to pick hit songs and American had completely missed the boat.

For years Hector had dreamed of the music business. He partly satisfied his ambition by purchasing a small radio station in Medillin. Against everyone's advice, he programmed American country music, exclusively. He also served as the station's program director, carefully choosing the playlist according to his intuitions. To everyone's surprise but his, the station was a big success, despite the language barrier. Country music, as Hector had predicted, was a natural for Colombians.

Because Sonny Boy was one of Hector's favorites, Mc-Daniel's records got extensive airplay in Medillin. In Medillin, his singles shot to the top of the chart and stayed there for weeks. When Hector's invitees had read that the evening's entertainment would be provided by Sonny Boy Mc-Daniel, they were genuinely excited. His presence at Hector's party would insure a good turnout. In Medillin, thanks to Hector, Sonny Boy was a big star.

An hour before the show, while the guests savored a banquet of royal proportions, Hector impatiently listened to Mason plead his case for a cancellation.

"Don Hector, please, listen to reason. Sonny Boy is in no condition to perform tonight. He's very sick. He doesn't comprehend his whereabouts. I'm afraid he'll embarrass you."

"Nothing would embarrass me more, Señor Reed, than a cancellation! I have gone to great trouble and expense. We built a stage, purchased a sound system and lighting. All to your specifications. The musicians have been practicing the songs for weeks. Tonight, my niece Esmeralda will sing with the great Sonny Boy McDaniel. She is thrilled. It would break her heart to cancel."

Carlos spoke from behind Mason, "Sí, Señor Reed. To cancel the show would break my daughter's heart."

Hector continued, "I have invited Medillin's elite, and the response has been wonderful. Certain people who have never come to La Ponderosa are here tonight. And they are here to be entertained by Sonny Boy McDaniel. How do you say it in America? The show must go on!" Hector laughed heartily, pleased with himself for his use of American slang.

Mason shifted gears. "Okay, Hector. Now hear the truth. Sonny Boy doesn't know anything about you. I realize it might be hard for you to understand, but in my country, you're not a king, you're a criminal. Public enemy number one. If I had been honest with McDaniel about you, he might have gone to the authorities, maybe the ones you don't control. We brought him here under false pretenses. In fact, we drugged him. Unfortunately, my idiot bodyguard overdid it. Sonny's been unconscious since we arrived. We're lucky he's alive. He hasn't practiced the songs, some of which he hasn't sung in years. As his manager, I'm telling you he's in no shape to perform."

Hector stared coldly at Mason. His face reflected a mixture of hurt and anger. "Very well, Mason. You have made your point. I won't hold you or him responsible if the show goes badly. But, I insist we try. We will not cancel. We will not reschedule. If he can't finish the show, I'll address my guests and explain that Mr. McDaniel is ill. But he must walk out on the stage... in costume." Hector's tailor had duplicated the costume from Sonny Boy's album, Buy This Record or I'll Shoot You.

Knowing that Hector always had the last word, Mason nodded his assent and exited to attempt a miracle. Maybe, he hoped, the strong Colombian coffee would revive Sonny Boy's debilitated nervous system. After Mason left the room, Carlos shook his head and said with contempt, "Gringos." Then he spat at the floor.

◆

The cowboy hat was a little large but the rest of his cloth-

84

ing fit nicely. Thank God I lost that weight, he thought. He touched the two revolvers strapped in holsters to his side. He pulled one out. It was heavy, too heavy for his sore arm. He noticed it wasn't loaded.

The makeup artist powdered his nose. She was young and pretty and she looked Mexican. He mumbled some fractured Spanish to her but she didn't respond. In all his life, he had never felt this way, like he was underwater. Maybe back in the seventies when he did all those Quaaludes. That's it, 'ludes. But he couldn't recall taking Quaaludes.

Mason appeared before him. He looked worried. "Okay, Sonny Boy, it's almost show time. If you pull this off, I'll buy you a new car. Any car you want."

"What? A new car? Where am I, Mason?"

Mason shook his head and released a loud sigh. Margo kissed Sonny Boy and wished him good luck. He heard someone speaking Spanish over the sound system. Then he heard his name spoken several times with enthusiasm. He heard music. Mason pushed him onto the stage. He walked unsteadily to the microphone. The lights were blinding, but he could see cowboy hats in the audience. He heard gunshots. More gunshots. He could see dozens of men in the audience shooting pistols in the air as they hooted and hollered. The band behind him was playing a song he had recorded years ago, one of his favorites. The musicians grinned at him. He moved closer to the mic. He began to sing, and somehow, someway, he remembered the words, at least, most of them. After all, he had sung this tune hundreds of times, years ago. He looked to his right. An angelic girl with long black hair sang harmony with him. She was good. He gave an inspired performance, gaining confidence with each song, reveling in the crowd's love for him. They demanded three encores. It was like a dream. A lovely dream.

EIGHTEEN

A soft knocking on the door woke him. Sonny Boy sat up and said, "Come in!" Two waiters dressed in white uniforms entered, one pushing a food tray.

"Good morning, Señor McDaniel. Are you ready for breakfast?"

He rubbed his eyes. For the first time in three days he felt normal, except for a slight headache. "Yeah, bring it on in. I'm kinda hungry. Whatcha got there?"

"Grilled marlin. Scrambled eggs with crabmeat topping. Fruit salad. Orange juice I squeezed myself and croissants from our own bakery. And, of course, Señor, a pot of our famous Colombian coffee. Does your breakfast meet with your approval?"

Sonny Boy sat up in bed and surveyed the feast before him. He blew his nose on the bedsheet and asked, "Got any bacon?"

"Bacon? Sí, Señor, sí. Of course." He addressed the other waiter in Spanish, "José, bring Señor McDaniel a dozen strips of bacon. Be quick!" José left hurriedly.

Sonny Boy liked the snappy service he was receiving. "Thanks. Say, partner, can you tell me where I am?"

The head waiter looked puzzled and did not respond, but shook his head, dumbfounded. Sonny repeated his question. "Old timer, I said can you tell me where I am? I've lost my bearings."

"Señor McDaniel, you are at La Ponderosa. You are our special guest. Last night you performed for us. You were very good. Three encores. Bravo! I liked most the song, 'Raylene, My Trailer Park Queen'."

"Oh yeah? 'Raylene'? Good. I always thought that should have been a hit. Too bad my record company didn't agree. Tell me, before you leave, where is this La Ponderosa?"

Suddenly, the man's face changed. He looked worried and uncertain. "You better eat now. Food will make you feel better. Then you'll get back your memory. You've been sick. The bacon will be here soon. Before I go, I'll turn on the radio. You'll like it. Today is Sonny Boy McDaniel Day on Don Hector's radio station. All day, nothing but Sonny Boy. Listen!"

He turned on a large portable radio-cassette player. A song from an album Sonny Boy had recorded years ago was playing. Damn, Sonny Boy thought, imagine that.

The man continued, "All day long, Sonny Boy. Nothing but Sonny Boy. All in honor of you, our guest. Excuse me now, I must go."

After the door was closed, Sonny Boy heard a bolt click. He moved the breakfast tray and tried to open the door, but it was locked from the outside. Strange, he thought. He felt panicky. He went to the radio and turned the dial, searching for a clue to his whereabouts. He heard nothing but Spanish, except for an old American pop tune and the non-stop Sonny Boy McDaniel. He thought he was in Acapulco. Once, several years ago, he had played Acapulco. Guess they brought me back, he reasoned. He tuned the radio back to the station playing his music. When the song ended, he heard a Spanish speaking disc jockey introduce another of his more obscure recordings. He heard his name spoken with enthusiasm. "Damn-nation," he whispered, "Sonny Boy McDaniel Day in Acapulco."

He was hungry and ate ravenously. The bacon arrived, a

dozen perfect strips. He drank four cups of the best coffee he'd ever tasted. He was beginning to feel good. He heard another knock on his door, this time, louder. The bolt clicked, and a man entered, another Hispanic.

"Good morning, Señor McDaniel. I am Carlos, Hector's brother. Hector would like to go horseback riding with you this morning. Can you ride a horse, señor?"

Sonny Boy sensed a tone of sarcasm in the man's question. "Sure, amigo. I love to ride horses. But, tell me, who in the hell is this guy Hector?"

Carlos shot an angry glance at Sonny Boy. "I'm referring to your host, Don Hector Armadas, and, I should add, the man you work for." Carlos was holding a riding whip which he raised and pointed ominously at Sonny Boy.

"Never heard of him," Sonny Boy scoffed as he took a bite of scrambled eggs. He assumed Hector was a club owner in Acapulco, a big fish in a little pond.

"I suggest you finish your meal and get dressed. You will find riding clothes in the closet. They should fit you. A valet will come for you in one hour. Have a nice ride, señor." Then, with his riding whip, Carlos pushed over the half filled glass of orange juice on Sonny Boy's tray. The juice spread slowly over the tray as Carlos waited for McDaniel's response.

What a jackass, Sonny Boy thought. Local jerks are all the same, even in Mexico. What's his problem? He decided to ignore the provocation and play the good sport. No problem. He smiled and Carlos left.

In exactly one hour the valet appeared and drove him in a golf cart to the stables. On the way, Sonny Boy was struck by the beauty of the grounds. He counted a score of gardeners working, including several Asians. He asked the valet, "Tell me, hoss, I've never heard of the La Ponderosa. Is it a new hotel? Who runs it? Marriott? Radisson?"

The valet shook his head. *"No comprendé. No anglais."*

Several attendants were waiting for him at the stables. A blonde six-footer introduced himself as Gunther. He spoke with a pronounced German accent.

"Mr. McDaniel, as you can see, vee have many horses to choose from. Tell me, sir, how often do you ride?"

"Well, to be honest, Gunther, I'm a little rusty." Sonny Boy winked. "Why don't you give me an easy one."

Gunther led him to a beautiful sandy colored Arabian, freshly brushed. "Herr McDaniel, meet Dolly Parton, a gentle mare. I think she'll do nicely for you."

Sonny Boy said, "I'll take her! I always wanted to ride Dolly Parton. Say, that's a funny name for a horse."

"Don Hector has named all his horses after country music stars. He's a big fan. Today, I believe he's riding... Villie Nelson."

Gunther helped Sonny Boy mount Dolly Parton and led him down a trail where Hector waited. Hector greeted Sonny Boy and then galloped away. Dolly followed Willie and Sonny Boy held on tightly. The men rode to the top of a hill overlooking La Ponderosa, dismounted, and tied their horses to a small tree.

Hector extended his hand to Sonny Boy. "Señor McDaniel, permit me to introduce myself. I am Hector Armadas Galéna, at your service. Have you heard of me?"

Sonny Boy shook his head, "No sir, don't believe so. Do you own any clubs in the States?"

"No, I own many things in your country, but no night clubs. At least, I don't think I do. Did you sleep well?"

"Like a proverbial baby."

"Breakfast?"

"Delicious, Hector. You run a real classy joint. But tell me, where is the ocean? I assume we're in Acapulco."

Hector chuckled. "Sit down, amigo. It's time we had a good talk. *Mano a mano.*" Hector motioned toward two men on horses about twenty yards away, one of whom was holding a submachine gun. The other dismounted and brought two wooden folding chairs to Hector and Sonny Boy.

"Sonny Boy, first let me congratulate you on a wonderful show last night. You were *magnífico!* Mason wanted to cancel the show. I'm glad I insisted that you perform."

"Mason? Say, where is that turkey? Is he here?"

"Yes, of course. He's staying in the big house, my *hacienda.* Margo is also here. She's very anxious to see you." Hector grinned.

"Hector, where the hell am I? The last few days are a blur. I remember getting on a plane in Barbados... Hey, I got it! You're Mason's silent partner."

"Sí, sí. I *am* Mason's partner and you are my guest. And I dare say I am probably your biggest fan... in the whole world."

"Well, thank you, Hector. Thanks for your support. Mason hasn't told me much about you, but I understand you're a very wealthy man."

"Everything is relative, but I am a man of means."

"C'mon, hoss, tell me. Just how rich are you?"

Hector sighed at the typical *yanqui* brashness of such an inappropriate question. He replied, "A famous American once said, 'If you know how much you're worth, you're not worth much.' That's me. My wealth changes by the minute, but, thank God, it's always growing." Then, like a good Catholic, he made the sign of the cross.

"Mason claims you're a... billionaire."

Hector looked sheepish, as if accused of a minor transgression. "Sí, señor, and in dollars. Good old greenbacks. Although my wealth is invested in many currencies. You can't be too careful, you know."

Sonny Boy mumbled, "Right," and walked to the edge of the hill. He pointed at the red tiled roofs below them. "And I guess that's your hotel, the La Ponderosa? Is it a franchise?"

"Yes, it's mine. But it's not a hotel. It's my home. And, please, don't say *the* La Ponderosa. That's, how do you say, redundant?"

"Yeah, yeah. But that's your home?"

"Yes, my estate. Over ten thousand acres. I'm very proud of it. Elena and I—Elena is my wife—we have created our own world here." Hector walked to Sonny Boy's side. He pointed, "That's the main house where we live with my four children; the oldest is sixteen, the youngest is seven. They grow up so fast. Do you have children, Señor?"

Sonny Boy shook his head.

"Oh, too bad. Don't miss it. Having children is what it's all about. Over there are the guest cottages where you're staying. You can see the gardens, the tennis courts, the polo field. Three pools. Can you see the greens over there? That's the pin at number nine. Our course was designed by a very famous American golfer, who prefers to remain anonymous. Do you play?"

"Not too good."

"I certainly understand. I'm fighting a terrible slice. But, no matter. Tomorrow, weather permitting, you and I and Carlos, my brother, and Mason will make a foursome. Okay?"

"Sure, hoss. No problem. But you still haven't answered my question."

"What's that, Sonny Boy?"

"Where's the ocean?"

"The ocean is far away."

"This ain't Acapulco, is it?"

"No. It's not even Mexico."

Sonny Boy looked intently at Hector. He couldn't hide his fear completely. "So, where am I, Hector?"

Hector collected his thoughts and spoke deliberately, with a hint of pride. "You're outside Medillin, Colombia, the cocaine capital of the world, and I am the biggest processor and exporter of cocaine in the world, though my competitors in Cali are giving us a run for our money, as you say in the States. Tomorrow, if you like, after golf, I'll show you our plant where we take the coca paste we buy from our Bolivian suppliers and process it into cocaine. We don't actually grow coca here, they can do it cheaper in Bolivia. We're more like a bottling company. Our strength is distribution. But we pride ourselves on selling the finest cocaine in the world. The champagne of cocaine, I like to say."

Sonny Boy felt his face flush and a wave of nausea stirred the rich contents of his stomach. The enormity of his predicament struck him full force. He returned to his chair, shaken.

"Cocaine? You sell cocaine?" he asked meekly.

"Yes. Tons of it. And mostly in your country. We have a wonderful market there. Very strong, though somewhat cyclical. We work hard to satisfy the enormous worldwide demand for our product. And I'm proud to say, in doing so, we employ over a hundred people here at good wages, plus benefits. Not to mention the hundreds of Bolivian peasants we support. Around here, good jobs are hard to come by."

Sonny Boy sat in stunned silence. Hector pointed to the valley below. "Do you see that group of buildings over there?"

Sonny Boy nodded his head in the affirmative.

"Those buildings comprise a training school I operate."

"For what? Auto mechanics?"

Hector chuckled. "No. no. For *sicarios.*"

"What's that?"

"A *sicario* is a professional killer." Hector paused to allow the import of his message to sink into McDaniel's befuddled brain. "Presently, I employ about sixty *sicarios* posted all over the world. Several of my very best men are stationed in the U.S.A. My school is under the direction of Colonel Ed Green, a rather famous American mercenary. Have you heard of him?"

"No. I haven't. An American. Imagine that."

"Colonel Green was very active in Africa. He worked for Idi Amin. You should hear the stories! He's tough, a real macho son of a bitch. That's what I look for in my associates, *macho.* Like you, Sonny Boy, a tough guy. Buy this record or I'll shoot you. That was great. *Clasico.*"

Sonny Boy looked around for an escape. Impossible. The armed men were a short distance away, watching.

"Mr. Armadas, I appreciate your hospitality. I really do. I appreciate the fact that you like my music. I understand how much you're helping Mason and me, professionally speaking. But, I can't, I repeat, I cannot be involved with cocaine. No way, José."

Hector cut a sharp glance at Sonny, his eyes dark stones of dead hate. He waited for Sonny to continue.

"No disrespect meant, sir. But coke almost destroyed my life. It near 'bout killed me. Not to mention the fortune I blew up my nose."

Hector smiled. "But I don't want you to use cocaine, Sonny Boy. In fact, I forbid it. Cocaine is like fire, it must be used with extreme caution, with great discretion."

"Mr. Armadas, cocaine is bad. It causes so many problems in my country."

"Yes, there is abuse, I concede. But mainly with the

Blacks. The Blacks have very little self-control. They have no *discretion*."

"But, it's ... addictive."

"Yes, I agree. But so is nicotine. And just last year, I understand your tour was sponsored by Cowboy cigarettes. What's the difference? Tobacco kills many, many more people than our product."

"I'm not proud of my association with Cowboy. And, in fact, I am no longer affiliated with them."

"Oh, yes, I know. They dropped you. Face it, Sonny Boy. Unless you have a hit record soon, your career is finished. You won't have to concern yourself with the ethics of your sponsor because you won't have one." Hector motioned for his horse. "I suggest you ponder these matters carefully. In Colombia we have a saying, *plomo ó plata*."

"What does it mean?"

"Lead or silver. You can choose the lead bullet or the silver coin. It's your choice. Like the offer you can't refuse in the *Godfather* movies. Did you see them?"

"Sure."

"The first two were wonderful. Masterpieces. The third was a disaster. It should have never been made. Americans never know when to stop. Again, a lack of discretion." As Hector mounted his horse, he shouted to Sonny Boy, "Remember, my friend, *plomo ó plata*. Lead or silver. It's your choice, but you *must* choose."

Nineteen

As Tommy watched Susan returning from the ladies' room, he thought to himself, 'What in God's name am I doing here?' But he knew what he was doing—he was plying Susan with wine and friendship in an effort to get closer to Mason. It was fools' play, but he was determined to know the truth about Reed. Despite all the warning signs and his own instinct to run the other way, he was drawn to Mason, whose money and power worked on Tommy like a perverse form of gravity. The young man rationalized that once he had the goods on his employer, he would go to the FBI and shut the bastard down. Susan was the key. She had gotten him the job with Reed in the first place and she could, if she chose to, bring Tommy into the inner circle. And that's where he wanted to be. For whatever crazy or inspired, flimsy or rock solid reason he could think of, he wanted to move deeper into the mystery. A part of him wanted to look Armadas right in the eye.

Susan settled in her chair and smiled loosely at him. The waiter drained the last of the chardonnay, carefully dividing the wine between two glasses. "Sir, your entrees should be ready in a minute. Would you care for another bottle of wine?"

Tommy smiled at Susan. "Whadaya think kiddo? Can you handle another bottle?"

She grinned. "Why not? Let's go for it."

Tommy nodded at the waiter. "Bring us another bottle of the same." He lifted his glass to Susan. "A toast."

"Another toast? Let's see, we've toasted Nashville, the Grand Ole Opry, Elvis, the future, world peace, what's left?"

"Well... to us!"

"Okay, to... us." Susan almost blushed. She felt like a high school girl on prom night. Tommy had completely charmed her.

"Tommy, this wine is thirty dollars a bottle. I know what Mason pays you. Why don't you let me help you with the tab?"

"Of course not, mah deah," Tommy said, attempting his best Rhett Butler. "I wouldn't considah allowing mah lady to expend her own funds. It simply isn't done heah in the South."

"My, my. You are in rare form. I must say, I like it."

In the candlelight, Susan looked almost innocent. Tommy was sincerely fond of her, but tonight was strictly business. The waiter brought their dinners; tenderloin for Tommy, swordfish for Susan.

"Susan, before we begin, let me propose one last toast. Here's to you, my friend, Susan. Thanks for everything. If I hadn't met you... well, I'm just glad I did."

They clinked glasses. Tommy felt Susan's shoeless foot rub his leg.

"Tommy, really, you're shameless. I can't wait to get my hands on you."

After dinner, over coffee and dessert, Tommy popped the question he had been waiting to ask. "So, tell me, who *is* Mason Reed?"

Susan shook her head. "Oh, nooooo. Not Mason. I don't want to talk about Mason."

"Why not?"

"It bores me. It's complicated. Please, not tonight."

Tommy sat silently, waiting for her to continue. Susan

sighed. "Look, Mason is exactly as he appears. That's the secret of his power. He's brilliant and ruthless and... dangerous. The less you know about him, the better for you."

"But, Susan, do you love him? I mean, you live together."

Susan was startled by the directness of Tommy's question. "Yes, after a fashion I love him. We help each other. I don't have a family and neither does he. So, in a way, we're family. It's platonic, believe me! And that's all I want to say about it."

Tommy persisted despite her reluctance. "What do you mean, you don't have a family? Are you an orphan?"

"I guess you could put it that way. My parents disowned me several years ago. Let's just say they didn't approve of my lifestyle. We haven't communicated since. But... they live close to Nashville. In Atlanta."

Tommy detected real pain in Susan's voice. Her eyes reddened and watered. Through her polished, hard veneer, he saw that she, too, was a victim. He changed the subject.

"Well, what about Mason's family?"

"Mason is really alone. No brothers, no sisters. His father committed suicide when he was a boy. A few years later his mother was sent to an insane asylum. She died a couple of years ago. It's sad what life can dish out."

"Help me get closer to him," Tommy implored, as he leaned across the table. "Please?" He felt her foot leave his leg.

"Okay, Tommy. But remember, I warned you. Now shut up and pay the bill."

Tommy smiled and obeyed.

◆

Within a few days of his dinner with Susan, Tommy was summoned to Mason's office. On his way in Susan winked at him, and he knew this meeting was her gift to him. He seated himself and waited alone for Mason's arrival. He noticed an elegant black leather attaché case sitting on Mason's desk.

He waited. And waited. Finally, he heard Susan's voice over the speaker-phone.

"Tommy, Mason can't meet with you in person, but he wants to talk to you on the speaker-phone. Push the flashing button and sit tight."

"Price, are you there? This is Mason."

"Yes sir. I'm right here."

"Can you hear me clearly? What I have to say is important and extremely confidential."

Tommy's throat tightened. "Yes sir, I can hear you fine."

"Susan tells me you want to advance in the organization."

"Yes sir, that's right."

"Good. I'm pleased with your work at the House of Reed. Like I've told you, you think like a Jew. You see around corners. *Yiddiseh Kop*. That's rare in a goyim."

Tommy coughed. "Well, thank you Mr. Reed. I guess that's a compliment."

"Of course it's a compliment. I see around corners, too. Now tell me, are you interested in learning more about the record business?"

"Yes sir. Definitely."

"Well, so am I, Price, so am I. It might surprise you but I don't really understand the record business. Not like I should. And I don't know much about radio either, or how the two work together. Do you?"

Tommy felt unnerved conversing with a disembodied voice. "No sir, I don't understand records or radio. I want to learn."

"Good, Price. We'll learn together. If the record business is like other businesses, there's one thing that really counts. Know what that is?"

"Hard work?"

"No. Hard work helps, but it's not essential. Guess again."

"Talent?"

"No. Talent doesn't count for much. The world is full of talented losers. One more try."

Tommy squirmed in his chair, unsure where Mason was leading him with his questions. Then Mason bellowed, "Money, Price. It takes money to make money. In front of you, you should see a briefcase."

"Yes sir."

"Open it."

Tommy did as he was told. When the case opened, he froze. It was filled with crisp one hundred dollar bills, bundled and stacked neatly in rows.

"Price, are you there?"

"Ah, yes sir. I'm right here."

"And what do you see?"

"Money. Lots of it. Stacks of hundreds."

"There should be one hundred thousand dollars, unless Bobby got sticky fingers. Do you see a note in the case?"

"Yes sir."

"Read it."

The typed note was simply a list of radio stations with names, addresses, and phone numbers. All the stations were located in the eastern half of the country.

"Mr. Reed, all I see is a list of radio stations."

"That's right. Those are our target stations. These stations are not playing 'Wayward Angel.' If they don't add the record within the next two weeks, we'll lose our bullet. I am determined to make 'Wayward Angel' our first number one. Whatever it takes, Price. Do you understand? Whatever it takes."

"Yes sir, I understand."

"Price, why don't you take some time off? You've earned a vacation. Take Gus with you. Start today. Contact the people on that list. Persuade them to play 'Wayward Angel.' I think you and Gus can figure this thing out. Just remember one thing."

"What's that, Mr. Reed?"

"If you're so stupid as to get caught dealing payola, you take the fall. As of this moment, I know nothing about this. Got it?"

"Yes sir. I've got it."

"Okay. If there's nothing else, get to work."

For several minutes, Tommy stared at the money. He felt a strange calmness. He stood, closed the briefcase, picked it up, and left the office. Too late to turn back now, he thought, as the elevator descended Crown Tower.

TWENTY

The Cumberland Marina was a rather modest operation situated on Old Hickory Lake, a few miles east of Nashville. From this landlocked harbor, a determined sailor could reach the Gulf of Mexico via the Tenn-Tom Waterway. Most of the vessels in the marina were houseboats which never left the lake. But, the fact that the Gulf, and thus, the world, were accessible from there imbued the place with a faint romantic *ambiance*.

From a hill above the lake Jonetta surveyed the scene below, looking for the S.S. *Lollipop*, where she was to meet Ruby McDaniel for "a little chat." Jonetta had been contacted by Mavis Herndon, who had requested the meeting on Ruby's behalf and had made the arrangements. This, however, would not be Jonetta's first encounter with Ruby. They had had a brief but intimate visit a few months earlier returning from Talladega on Mason's party bus. At that time Ruby had displayed a genuine interest in Jonetta, intently inquiring about her background, family, education, ambitions, and dreams. Jonetta had been completely charmed by the legendary woman's attention, and they had agreed to continue the visit, another time, another place, sooner rather than later. When she had heard from Mavis she had assumed Ruby was as good as her word. Now, Jonetta hoped, I have found my entree to the country music establishment.

Jonetta spotted Ruby waving to her from the sundeck of a large, pale pink houseboat, and she made her way down the hill to the *Lollipop*. Once she was settled in a deck chair and fitted with an *S.S. Lollipop* crew cap, Ruby asked her, "Jonetta, what's your pleasure? Mavis makes a dangerous planter's punch. Cold beer? Co-cola? Ice tea? We've got it all on the good ship *Lollipop*. And if we don't have it, we'll get it."

Jonetta hesitated. "Oh, let's see, I think a beer sounds good."

Ruby went below to retrieve the beer. Jonetta could see that the *Lollipop* was unlike any craft she had ever boarded. Half a dozen cats roamed the premises. Potted plants, assorted bric-a-brac, and junk store exotica gave the boat the appearance of a floating yard sale. But, it felt homey, and Jonetta relaxed.

Ruby returned with the beer and a frosted mug. Then she shouted to Mavis, "Okay, captain, anchors aweigh! Let's give Jonetta the grand tour."

As they skimmed the surface of the placid, gray-green water, Jonetta felt a deep, forgotten part of herself revive. A few minutes from shore, Ruby offered her a life jacket. She declined. Jonetta was proud of her proficiency as a swimmer and was confident in and around water. She had been the first Black on the Vanderbilt women's swim team, and she relished her aquatic nature. Indeed, she had worn her swimsuit under her clothing in case she got the chance.

A late August sun began its afternoon descent as the motor calmed and the boat slowed to a crawl. They entered a cool, verdant cove. Mavis put the vessel in reverse for a moment and then shut down the engine. A preternatural silence bathed the scene, the only sound coming from the short waves lapping against the boat. Ruby disappeared again and returned with two cane fishing poles.

"Wanna drop a line? You never know, might hook a big one," Ruby asked Jonetta.

Jonetta giggled. She hadn't fished in many years. "Oh, I

don't think so. But I wish my mama could be here. She loves to fish and never gets to."

Ruby opened a white paper cup filled with black humus and plucked out a squirming, succulent earthworm. She expertly threaded her hook through the worm, despite the handicap created by her preposterously long, lavender fingernails.

"Are you sure you won't try? Never know. It's a shame to let a pole sit idle."

"Well, okay. But only if you'll bait it for me. I'm not good at that part."

Ruby smiled. "Used to be, we had to fish for the supper table. I bet your mama remembers those days. Young people don't know how far we've come and... how much we've lost."

Ruby threw Jonetta's fishing line over the side. The red and white bobber landed about two feet from an ancient, partially submerged oak tree.

"There you go. That should be a good spot." She handed the pole to Jonetta. After a half hour of watching their bobbers dance hypnotically on the surface without a bite, Ruby called for Mavis, who joined them.

"Fish ain't bitin'?" Mavis asked. Ruby grumbled in the negative. "Wanna try another spot?" Again, Ruby signified no.

Jonetta studied Mavis. She was a solid woman a few years past middle age. Her hair was cropped short and lightly frosted. She wore a Nashville Sounds baseball cap to shield her eyes, which were blue green and discerning. Her face was rough but serene, and she seemed comfortable with herself.

Without moving her gaze from her bobber, Ruby said solemnly, "Jonetta, Mavis has something to tell you. Listen up."

Mavis then spoke in a dispassionate manner about extraordinary things. "For many years I have studied a spiritual discipline called Astranetics. Are you familiar with it?"

"No. I've never heard of it," Jonetta replied.

"Astranetics is the science and religion of out of the body travel. Using contemplation and mind control, we learn to leave our bodies and travel to other planes of existence." She paused.

From the corner of her eye, Jonetta thought she saw her bobber dip below the surface, but ignored it, distracted by Mavis' amazing revelation.

"When we soul travel we go to places where we acquire spiritual wisdom and training. We can also observe earthly life from a higher plane. The other night I woke up from a vivid, terrifying dream, which I won't relate, except to say my dream was about Junior..."

"That's my son, Sonny Boy McDaniel," Ruby interjected.

"Junior was in trouble. Again. You see, I've had this dream before when Sonny was in a jam. I couldn't go back to sleep, so I got up and went to my meditation chair. Within a few minutes, I was out of my body, ready to travel."

"Out of your body? How do you mean?" Jonetta asked with a trace of incredulity.

"Our physical bodies are merely vehicles for our eternal souls. You should know that. In fact, at some level, you *do* know that. With proper technique and right motivation, a person can leave their earthly body and travel in this and other dimensions, utilizing the soul body or the astral body. This secret knowledge has been known and practiced by mystics for thousands of years. When we die, we all take a soul trip."

"Is it dangerous?"

"It can be. Evil exists on other planes as well. That's why right motivation is so important. When our purpose is good, we're protected."

Jonetta turned to Ruby. "Have you experienced soul travel?"

"No, honey. I leave all the spooky stuff to Mavis. But, sometimes when a young cowboy is doing ol' Ruby right, I feel like I'm hovering over my body..."

"Oh, Ruby, be serious!" Mavis demanded. "Anyway, Jonetta, I saw Sonny Boy lying in bed in a locked room, guarded by armed men. He was unconscious but he was struggling to wake up. I got the feeling he had been drugged. This happened during the time he was with Mason Reed in Barbados. But, he wasn't in Barbados."

"How do you know that?"

"Because the guards were speaking Spanish, and Barbados is an English speaking country."

"I see. So, what else did you... observe?"

"Before I returned to my body, I looked around a little. There were guns everywhere. Evil permeated the air. The place was luxurious, almost palatial, but it was rotten to the core. My main impression was that Sonny was in serious trouble, under the control of some bad people. Very bad people. I shudder now at the memory of it."

Ruby spoke. "Mavis told me about her vision. When Sonny Boy got home I could tell something was wrong. A mother knows. He had a fearful look in his eye. I asked him about the trip, but he wouldn't say much, which isn't like him. He hasn't been the same since that trip. Finally, a few days ago, he got tired of my nagging and he spilled the beans. Told us the whole, sorry story. That's why we called you. Do you remember our visit on the bus back from Talladega?"

"Yes, of course," Jonetta replied.

"You told me then you had heard some ugly rumors about Mason Reed. And, you said you were looking into them."

"I said that?"

Ruby and Mavis nodded their heads affirmatively in tandem.

"Oh, yes, those rumors. The ones about cocaine money?"

"Right," Ruby and Mavis answered in unison.

"Well, I haven't gone any further with my..."

"Jonetta, Sonny Boy confirmed those rumors to us," Ruby said. "He told us he had been drugged, kidnapped, taken to Colombia, and forced to do a concert..."

"Without compensation," Mavis added with emphasis.

"Yes, *without* compensation. And, he was threatened by a certain Hector Armadas, who told Junior he would kill him if he didn't cooperate."

Jonetta slumped in her deck chair. An overwhelming realization dawned on her—she was destined to pursue this story to its conclusion. She couldn't avoid it. Her dangerous opportunity both excited and repelled her, but it would not leave her alone.

The women talked another hour. Jonetta mentioned Tommy Price as a probable ally, someone on the inside. Sonny Boy was so afraid he had made his mother and Mavis promise they wouldn't contact the police. Despite the questionable wisdom of that promise, they decided to honor it, for the time being. They agreed to meet again within a week. After their intense conversation, Jonetta felt drained, confused, and a little dirty.

"How deep is it here?" she asked Ruby, pointing to the lake.

"Oh, it's deep. About forty feet."

Jonetta removed her shoes, shorts and t-shirt and stood before them, an exquisite young woman in her prime. From the upper deck she executed a perfect dive into the passive waters of Old Hickory Lake, then swam with strong strokes away from the boat and floated on her back. For a long time she watched the changing clouds above her, alone with her thoughts.

TWENTY ONE

Through a foggy September night, the black PNR limousine hurtled northward on Interstate 71, about a hundred miles from Columbus, Ohio. A luminous plastic angel swung from the rearview mirror. Gus brought the Christmas ornament for luck and as a reminder of the trip's purpose. The redolent odor of reefer filled the vehicle as Tommy puffed a fat one. He offered the joint to Gus.

"No, thanks. That would put me to sleep, and we'd end up in a ditch... or worse." Gus lit a cigarette instead and pressed the accelerator. The huge Cadillac responded sluggishly.

Tommy twisted the radio dial, searching for country music. Outside of Louisville they had heard the second half of "Wayward Angel." Tommy wanted to feel that thrill again. The song was a success where it was being played. But, it was doomed to be another near-miss for Sonny Boy unless Mason's targeted stations added it to their playlists. In the trunk the briefcase containing $98,000 lay waiting under an Army blanket, its covert power imminently available. Gus and Tommy had appropriated one thousand dollars each for expenses. Tommy had already spent part of his share on the cannabis he had bought to "calm his nerves."

"Oh Gus... Gus... Gus," Tommy moaned as the marijuana loosened his tongue.

"What is it, kiddo?"

"Oh man, what's it all about? What's it all for? What's the damn point?"

"Of what, son?"

"Of anything. Of everything. Of nothing," he sighed.

"Tommy, you're waxing poetic. Keep it up and know what you get?"

"What?"

"Waxy poetic buildup. Bad for the brain. A serious condition."

"Very clever," Tommy said glumly.

"Why so ... philosophical?"

"Why? Cause here I am, in the middle of nowhere, out on this metaphorical highway of life, chasing a pipe dream, preparing myself to commit a string of felonies that could put me away until ... "

"Until?"

"Until I'm as old as you are."

"That hurt."

"Sorry. I'm just having second thoughts."

"Tommy, don't do this thing for me. I can drop you off at the airport in Columbus. With or without you, I'm in. If it takes paying off some know-nothing yuppie jerks to get my song played, then by God, I'll do it. Like you said, I'm an old man. I've got nothing left to lose. Maybe you got too much to lose."

Again, Tommy drew deeply on the joint. "Sorry Gus, I'll stop bitching. Hell, I got you into this whole mess. I'm not going to let you down. Anyway, I want to know the truth."

"The truth? About what?"

"The truth about how hit records are made. The truth about ... myself. We're going into the belly of the beast, the heart of darkness."

Then, through the static they heard the opening bars of

"Wayward Angel." The DJ said, "Here's the new one from Sonny Boy McDaniel!" For three minutes and thirteen seconds they said nothing, savoring every moment of the sweetest experience a songwriter can have. When the song ended the announcer said, "Looks like ole Sonny Boy finally has himself a hit. The phones really light up when we play that one. We'll feature it again before midnight."

"Hot damn!" Tommy shouted. "Didya hear that? The phones are ringing. Bingo. It's a hit. He said it, it's a hit."

Despite skepticism born of a thousand disappointments, Gus' weathered face broke into a broad grin. "Yeah. Amen. Thank you, Jesus! What station is that?"

Tommy checked the dial. "One oh one point three. Not on our list. The signal is weak. Probably a secondary. Who cares? Man, I'm so excited I feel like I wrote the damn thing."

The men exchanged a spirited high five. Tommy opened the glove compartment and removed Mason's list. "Tomorrow at ten, first stop, WXNZ. Michael Innis is the program director. He's mine!"

On the outskirts of Columbus they found a Holiday Inn. Tommy was asleep within moments of lying down. Gus, however, restless and keyed-up, went out to the limo and tuned the radio to a very faint one oh one point three. He fell asleep on the back seat, waiting to hear his song again. That night he dreamed of a girl he had loved many years ago, when he was young and full of hope.

◆

S. Michael Innis kept them waiting over an hour in the lobby of WXNZ. Finally, an unsmiling girl sporting a nose ring escorted them to Innis' office, a cramped, messy cubicle with no place to sit.

"Sorry, guys. Monday morning's a bitch." Innis appeared a couple years past voting age. In spite of his youth and the early hour, he seemed exhausted. "So, I understand you guys are from Eagle. New kid on the block. Or should I say *row*? Ha! Get it? New kid on the row. What have you got? But please, gentlemen, make it quick. Time is a precious commodity around here."

"I'm Tommy Price and this is Gus Rogers. We drove all the way from Nashville to personally persuade you to add 'Wayward Angel.' And, by the way, Gus wrote the song."

"Oh yeah? Good song. But good songs are a dime a dozen."

"This is a *great* song. It's a hit," Tommy said emphatically.

"No offense, man, but it's a hit if we make it a hit. Know what I mean?" Innis was no pushover.

"But, we *know* it's a hit. When people hear it, they love it. The phones light up."

"Who says?" Innis was cocky to the point of arrogance.

"Well, the jock at one oh one point three. He was raving about it last night as we drove in."

"Yeah, yeah. I know that bozo. I used to work at that station when I was in high school. A secondary. The Z machine is in a different league. We're very selective about the records we play."

Tommy leaned closer to Innis, "Mike, have you actually heard the record?"

"Please, I prefer Michael. And actually, I haven't personally reviewed it, but I overheard someone say it was a good song. Someone I respect. The problem isn't the song. It's Sonny Boy McDaniel. He's a little long in the tooth for our image. Our motto is 'Rockin' Young Country.' Sonny Boy ain't rockin' and he ain't young."

Tommy pressed on. "Adam Speer, who was chosen Producer of the Year by *Rolling Stone*, well, he produced it."

"Oh, yeah? He's cool. What's he doing in Nashvegas? Must need the money."

Gus finally spoke, "Michael..."

"Yes sir?"

"Tell me, son, if you haven't actually heard the record, how can you be so sure it's *not* a hit?"

"Good question. To be honest, you see, I don't make the final, I mean, ultimately, the decision whether to play a particular record... isn't mine to make."

"They told us you were the man to see. The program director. If it ain't you, who is it?" Gus' voice had an edge that could cut paper.

"I *am* the program director." He handed Gus a business card as proof. "But the station employs a consultant. And I rely on his advice. Heavily."

"A consultant?"

"Right. He does research, polling, focus groups, etcetera. Then he tells us what to play. It's real scientific."

Tommy pulled out Mason's list. "Michael, would you look over this list? Do these stations also use a consultant?"

Innis studied the information. "Yep, all of these stations use the same consultant, Ernie Cox. And Ernie's negative on the record... based on his research."

"Ernie Cox?"

"Right."

"Where can we find him?"

"He lives in the Sea Pines Plantation on Hilton Head Island. That's in South Carolina. Nice place. Every year he throws a big, three day party for all his clients. It's wild. *Real* wild." Innis rolled his eyes at some private memory.

Gus asked, "So, Ernie Cox is the man to see?"

"Right, he controls a lot of radio stations. Without him on board, a record cannot reach the top twenty. It's that simple."

"You mean one man can make or break a record?" Tommy asked.

"Yep, one man. Mr. Ernie Cox."

◆

With little discussion, Gus and Tommy began the long drive to South Carolina. Every hundred miles or so, they called the number Innis had provided. No secretary took the calls, and Cox's recorded message was short and sweet. 'This is Ernie. At the beep, speak.' Gus considered it odd that a big time operator ran such a low rent operation. He suspected they were chasing a wild goose and persuaded Tommy to stop at another station on their list in Virginia. There, the program director echoed the story they had heard in Ohio, convincing them Cox was the key.

"I feel like we're off to see the wizard," Gus said.

"Yeah. This whole thing gets weirder the deeper we go. Maybe Cox won't be there. I'd hate to go back to Nashville empty-handed. Mason is one man I don't want to disappoint."

"You got that right."

Tommy pushed the dangling angel, causing it to swing in a wide circle.

"Do you believe in angels?" he asked Gus.

"Yeah. Definitely."

"Why?"

"When my mother died, she opened her eyes, sat bolt right up in bed and said, 'I'm going home. The angels are here.' Then she fell back, deader'n hell. Last words she ever spoke. But that look on her face. Pure joy. She must've seen something."

"I wasn't with my mother when she died. I was at school. She was raised Catholic. I think she believed in angels, but she never said so."

"Are you Catholic?"

"No, I'm nothing."

"Nothing?"

"I don't know what I believe in, if anything." Tommy grabbed the angel and stopped its swinging motion. "Gus, I have a confession. I'm half Jewish."

Gus was taken aback. "Price ain't no Jew name."

"My real name is Friedman. Price is my middle name, my mother's maiden name." An uncomfortable silence ensued. Tommy realized that if Gus was anti-semitic, their friendship would wither. It had happened before to Tommy. "Does it bother you? Do you care that I'm Jewish?"

"Hell no. I take people one by one. But why do you hide it?"

"Hey, man, it's a show business tradition. And Nashville is the buckle on the Bible Belt. I thought it was best to keep it private."

"No wonder you're confused."

"Damn right. I'd like to believe in angels. Hell, I'd like to believe in Jesus Christ. Nice guy. But see what they did to him. Nailed that sucker to a cross. Nice guys finish last. Bad guys get ahead. Look around. Look at yourself. You're a nice guy..."

"And a loser? Is that what you're saying? Jesus asked, What does it profit a man to gain the world only to lose his soul? Good question. He also said the last shall be first. So, there's hope for guys like me... and you. Someday, maybe the nice guys will lead the parade. Might as well accept it, kid, you're one of us. A nice guy."

Gus grinned his crooked smile and Tommy felt better. They reached Savannah around midnight and crashed at a Motel Six.

◆

The next morning, they waited in line to enter the Sea Pines Plantation, oblivious to events in Colorado that would change everything. To their surprise, the guard informed them that Cox was expecting them. They were given directions and a yellow pass to hang on the rearview mirror. Cox lived at the end of Mockingbird Lane in a three-story beach house.

A deeply tanned, baby-faced man wearing a screaming Hawaiian shirt, flip-flops, and white shorts answered the door. "What took y'all so long? Come on in." When they reached the living room, Ernie Cox reclined on a sofa and resumed watching a football game on a widescreen television. One wall was covered with photographs of Ernie fraternizing with big names in country music and several prominent politicians. Gold and platinum albums covered another wall. A sweeping view of the Atlantic ocean lay beyond a hardwood deck.

"Have a seat, boys. I got ten grand on this game. Six point spread. The Falcons are down ten with three minutes to go."

A bikinied blonde pranced through the room, checking out the new arrivals.

"Baby, get these boys a beer," Ernie said out of the side of his mouth.

"That's okay, Mr. Cox. It's a little early," Tommy said politely.

"Suit yourself." He nodded at the girl and she disappeared. "Now, wha'cha'll got for Big Ernie?"

Tommy took the lead. "Whatever it takes, Ernie. We got it or we can get it. Just add 'Wayward Angel.'"

Ernie listened and waited for more.

Gus was in no mood for games, so he got right to the point. "Ernie, we brought $98,000. It's yours if all your stations add the single."

Ernie muted the game. He seemed heavy with fatigue. "Are y'all trying to bribe me? Boys, that's illegal. Sumpin' called pay-o-la. Ever heard of it?"

Tommy spoke deferentially, "Mr. Cox, we can't go back to Nashville without giving this thing our best shot. From all accounts, you're the man. You tell us what you want. We're here to do whatever it takes to make 'Wayward Angel' a hit."

"Save your money. We gave that record the green light this morning."

"You what?"

"Had to," Ernie mumbled.

"Why did you have to?"

"Y'all haven't heard, have you?"

"Heard what?"

"Sonny Boy McDaniel was murdered last night. Somewhere out west. Shot in the head. Terrible thing."

Gus and Tommy sat in stunned silence.

"Yep. Ol' Sonny Boy's departed this vale of tears. We added the record in honor of his memory. It was the right thing to do. I predict it'll go number one. Gettin' iced was a great career move for McDaniel. Too bad he won't be around to enjoy it."

The game ended with Atlanta losing by seven. Ernie slapped his thigh. "Goddamn Falcons. One point. Well, maybe I'll make it back on the Steelers. Say, you boys look a little pale. Are you ready for that beer? A little smoke?

Whatever you want, Ernie's got it." Ernie pressed his fore-finger to his nose and snorted.

"No thanks, Ernie. We better get back to Nashville," Tommy muttered.

"Aren't y'all forgetting sumpin'?" Ernie grinned.

"What?"

"Thank me for adding that record. Isn't that what you wanted?"

Gus shook his head. "Not this way, Ernie. Not this way."

TWENTY TWO

The Crown Tower conference room was packed with reporters, photographers, and minicam operators. Reluctantly, Mason had called a news conference to discuss Sonny Boy's death, the details of which titillated the nation. Rumors and speculations raced through the press corps, which was covering an unprecedented event, the execution-style murder of a country music star.

Mason delayed his entrance until Susan confirmed that CNN had arrived. He straightened his carefully chosen tie as Susan brushed dandruff from his dark suited shoulders. He took several deep breaths and exhaled loudly. Then he strode into the room like a Desert Storm general. The television lights startled and blinded him. He groped for his chair, his bravado suddenly misplaced, but he quickly regained his composure.

"Ladies and gentlemen, thank you for coming. My name is Mason Reed. I'm the president of Eagle Records, the label for which Mr. McDaniel recorded. I also served as Sonny Boy's personal manager." He cleared his throat and paused to sip a glass of ice water. "All of us here at Eagle are profoundly shocked and saddened by this horrible event. Early this morning I spoke with Dewayne Martin, Mr. McDaniel's road manager, who was with Sonny Boy when he died. According to Mr. Martin, shortly after 1:30 A.M. this morning, that's Rocky Mountain time, Mr. McDaniel's bus was about an hour outside of Denver headed for Dallas. Sonny Boy had done a show in Denver. By the way, I understand it was sold out. He was en route to play a rodeo in Dallas tonight. The driver heard a siren and the bus was pulled over by a Colorado Highway Patrol car. Two men dressed as patrolmen instructed the occupants of the bus to exit. This took several minutes since some of the band and crew members were asleep. Sonny Boy was the last person to leave the bus. The men said they wanted to question Sonny Boy and they escorted him to the patrol car. Once inside, they departed at a high rate of speed in the direction of Denver. After about fifteen minutes, when they didn't return, the crew became alarmed and gave chase. About five miles up the road they saw Mr. McDaniel stretched out in the middle of the highway. They narrowly missed running over him. He had been shot at least twice, once in the chest, and once," Mason took another sip of water, "... and once in the mouth." The crowd gasped. Someone moaned, "Oh, no!"

"At that point, Sonny Boy still had a faint pulse. His crew got him on his bus and phoned for help. They began the trip back to Denver, but, within minutes, Sonny Boy McDaniel died. The time of death was approximately two A.M. Presently, his body is in Denver. An autopsy has been performed. The results are not yet available. His body will be transported back to Nashville for burial. No other arrangements have been made. He leaves his wife, Tina, who we learned last week is pregnant with their first child," (another moan from the crowd) "and, of course, his mother, the great Ruby McDaniel. Our heartfelt condolences are extended to them and to all his family and many friends. This is a very sad day for all of us. And now, I'll take a few questions."

The room exploded. Mason's attention was drawn to a familiar face on the front row. He pointed to her.

"Mr. Reed, Jonetta Jordan, Channel Six. The details of this shooting are very strange. Do you think the Colorado Highway Patrol murdered Sonny Boy McDaniel?"

"Miss Jordan, I assume the state of Colorado is not about the business of murdering innocent people, especially celebrities."

"Then what's your explanation?"

"I don't *have* an explanation. I'm as baffled as anyone. Apparently, robbery wasn't the motive. It appears he was assassinated."

"Assassinated! Did he say assassinated?" a voice shouted. As the room approached bedlam, Mason instantly regretted his choice of words. Jonetta persisted.

"Mr. Reed, we've heard rumors that Sonny Boy had some serious drug problems. Could there be a connection?"

"No!" Mason shouted. "Absolutely not. McDaniel's drug problems were in his past. I have no personal knowledge that Sonny Boy was involved with drugs. Maybe the motive was ... political."

"Political?"

"Yes, Miss Jordan, political. This is a dangerous world we live in. Sonny Boy was a proud patriot. There are forces in the land which would silence a voice for God and country. I just don't know. In fact, I think it's best we end this news conference. *Now.* We'll release a written statement later today. Thank you." Mason quickly left the room, having whipped up a frenzy of speculation, quite contrary to his intention.

As the other journalists hurried to exit, Jonetta remained seated and fingered her engagement ring. Her mind cracked with thoughts of drugs, murder, and conspiracy. She checked her notebook for Ruby's number. She had it. Poor Ruby and Mavis. They had seen it coming. They must be devastated. She looked for Tommy's number. She had that, too. Good.

◆

For the first time since moving to Nashville, Mason left work early, exhausted by the press conference and the strain of dealing with Sonny Boy's murder. Since Gus was on the road with Tommy, Mason asked Susan to drive him home. She took the long way, choosing the backroads rather than the interstate. Early autumn had arrived in Middle Tennessee, and the trees were turning. In a few weeks a dozen shades of red and yellow would wash across the hills and blaze against the sky.

"I like the trees here," Mason said softly. "In L.A. we didn't have these trees. No seasons. I guess we'll find out what winter is like. Maybe it'll snow. That would be nice. All these hills covered with snow. All clean and white."

"Mason, you do realize we're in deep shit, don't you?" Susan asked coldly.

"Maybe I'll get a couple of sleds. I'll name mine Rosebud, and yours..."

"Earth to Mason! Did you hear me? We're in serious trouble. Why in God's name did you let them do it? Jesus, Mason, murder?!"

"When we got back from Medillin we put Sonny on around-the-clock surveillance. Hector insisted. We discovered that McDaniel had made an appointment with the U.S. Attorney for the day after tomorrow. From the phone taps, we knew he was freaking out. He was gonna sing. Excuse the pun. I tried to think of an alternative. I couldn't. Hector ordered it. Not me. They were his men. His best men. I had no way to stop it."

"So, you did know?"

Mason answered in a flat, depressed voice. "Yes, I knew. Not where, not when, not how. But I knew."

"You bastard. You son of a bitch! I never signed on for murder. The rest of it was almost fun: the petty corruption, bending the rules, the drugs, the sex. But this, never. Now we're all going down. Way down."

Mason patted her hand. "Maybe not, Suzy Creamcheese. Maybe not. The game isn't over yet." Mason looked at the hills, and his thoughts turned back to sleds and snow and *Citizen Kane.*

TWENTY THREE

On their way back to Nashville Gus and Tommy heard "Wayward Angel" past counting. The news of Sonny Boy's murder was all over the country music airwaves. Stations devoted large segments of time to retrospectives of his career, elevating him overnight from a has-been to a legend. There were skeptics, however. One caller suggested Sonny Boy had faked his death for the sake of publicity and predicted his reemergence after his record went number one. The announcer assured the public that, just like Elvis, Sonny Boy had joined that all-star choir in hillbilly heaven.

Sonny Boy's death also generated interest in Ruby, and her venerable recordings were retrieved from the vaults and played widely. The strangest moment occurred when a station in Alabama featured Ruby's obscure album cut, "The Sun Shines in My Sonny Boy's Eyes." As the maudlin paean unfolded, Gus sheepishly admitted that he, in fact, had written the song.

"You never told me you wrote a song about Sonny Boy. Man, this is creepy," Tommy said.

"I'm embarrassed about it."

"Why? It didn't sound too bad. Pretty corny, but I heard a lot of Gus Rogers in it. I kinda liked it. Gave me goosebumps."

"Yeah, the song's okay. I'm embarrassed 'cause I sold it to Ruby. *All* of it. She even put her name on it as the writer."

"What? You sold it? Why would you ever sell a song... a hundred percent?"

"Five thousand dollars, that's why. In 1965, five thousand was a lot of money. Especially in *my* 1965. Bad year. One of my divorces. I had to pay off number two. Anyway, I wrote it on assignment. Ruby needed a song to do in her show when the boy came out on stage. The crowds loved it."

"Like I said, it gave me goosebumps."

"Damn thing'll be a hit now. Like I keep telling you. Learn from my mistakes. Don't ever sell a song outright. Willie Nelson did it early in his career."

"Which one?"

"'Night Life', I think."

"Ouch."

As they crossed the state line at Chattanooga, the impending peril of their situation reasserted itself. Their thoughts returned to Sonny Boy's murder.

"They killed him, you know," Tommy whispered.

"Yeah, you're right I reckon. It had the markings of a hit."

"In the mouth."

"Yeah, in the mouth. This damn business is getting hazardous for a man's health. Payola, murder. Whole thing stinks. I got a mind to head down to Mexico. Live on my mailbox money from 'Angel.' The dollar goes a long way south of the border. Might last 'til I pass over."

"Yeah, Mexico sounds inviting."

"We could split the payola money we didn't use," Gus suggested.

"Get real, Gus. We're sure as hell not going to steal Mason's money. Even if it's drug money or whatever. I'm sure those Colorado cops could and would find us anywhere."

"It ain't like stealin', kid. Mission accomplished. Every

station on the list has added the record. Ernie said so. We earned it."

Tommy looked hard at Gus. "Old man, listen to me. We're giving all the money back. I won't let you make *that* mistake."

"Okay. But Mexico still sounds good. I just hate going back to Nashville. Bad things are happening there. Call it a hobo's intuition."

"Whatever. Gus, I need to whiz. Find a truck stop, will ya? I could use a burger, too."

◆

The waitress had burnt orange hair and a generous bosom. Her name tag read Myrtle. She smiled a gap toothed grin at Gus and called him 'sugar' twice, once with feeling.

"Gus, I've got to hand it to you. You do have a way with the ladies," Tommy said with approval.

"I confess. Girls like me. Always have. Did you know that gap tooth is a sign of passion in a woman?"

"C'mon now."

"Hey, who's the expert around here? Myrtle is a lusty wench, trust me."

"I'll keep it in mind." Instead, Jonetta came into his mind. He hadn't thought of her in days. He had enjoyed the respite from her mental intrusions. Now he realized that Sonny Boy's murder would affect her, too.

"God, I hope she doesn't do anything stupid," Tommy said.

"Who boy? Myrtle?"

"No, no. Jonetta."

"Oh, yeah. Her." Gus lit a cigarette. Silently, as he inhaled, he said a prayer for Jonetta. And one for Tommy. And then one for himself. "I'm telling you kid. Mexico ought to be our next stop. Hell, we can mail the briefcase back to Reed, money and all."

Tommy was disappointed in Gus. Gus wanted to run. Maybe there's a reason his friend was broke, broken and alone. Maybe he was a coward. He looked closely at Gus. Each line in his face seemed deeper, sadder. His two day beard was no longer charming; it seemed unkempt. Why won't he shave? I shave every day. His father had taught him, gentlemen shave twice a day. Gus' dirty fingernails needed clipping and his tobacco stained fingers were revolting. Tommy was seeing his partner in a new, unflattering light. Was he seeing himself twenty-five years hence? Suddenly, he stood.

"Be back in a minute. I got to pee. Order me a cheeseburger, okay? No. On second thought, don't. I lost my appetite." Tommy went to the restroom. It was filthy and reeked with an acrid odor. The urinal was out of order, filled with cigarette butts. He opened the stall. Jesus, can't these animals learn how to flush? He flushed the toilet and fought the urge to throw up. And then he did throw up, again and again, in violent spasms. He fell to his knees on the dirty, wet floor and dry-heaved. He heard someone enter the restroom. It was Gus.

"Are you okay, kid? What's wrong?" Gus helped him to his feet. He felt Gus' coarse hand on his forehead. "Man, you're burning up".

"I don't feel well."

"I guess not. Must be a stomach virus. Here, let's clean you up and get you home. We're only an hour from Nashville."

"I'm a little dizzy. Thanks."

When Tommy got home he checked his answering machine. Jonetta had called several times, frantic to speak with him. Careful, JJ, for God's sake, be careful. Susan had also called, sternly instructing him to report in immediately upon his arrival. His head pounded and his stomach groaned. Gus gave him two Advil and a Seven-up, then left. He sat in the only decent chair in his tiny apartment and stared blankly at the black briefcase as if it contained the source of all earthly evil.

TWENTY FOUR

On a gray Sunday afternoon, within twenty-four hours of their return to Nashville, Gus and Tommy sat on the circular sofa in Mason's sunken living room, fidgeting like truants in the principal's office. Mason had summoned them to a four o'clock meeting. On his lap Tommy held the briefcase.

"Hey, kid," Gus whispered.

"Yeah."

"Gotta smoke?"

"Yeah. But I don't see an ashtray. Maybe we shouldn't." They surveyed the room for an ashtray. Once entertained, the prospect of a cigarette induced a craving in both men. Bobby stood by the picture windows, watching them impassively. Tommy detected a bulge under Bobby's jacket and assumed it was a pistol.

"Hey, Bobby, is it okay to smoke?" Gus asked politely. Bobby shifted his weight but didn't reply.

Gus forcefully reiterated his question. "I said, Bobby, is it okay to smoke? Are you deaf?"

Tommy saw the color gathering in Gus' face. He tried to dispel the escalating tension. "We'll just go outside," he suggested.

"Don't go nowhere. Sit right there," Bobby said firmly.

"Well, I'll be damned. He can talk," Gus said sarcastically.

Then Mason and Susan entered the room with a frightened, tearful Jonetta Jordan between them.

"My God, Jonetta!" Tommy blurted as he jumped to his feet.

"Sit down, Price," Mason ordered. "Bobby, take the briefcase from him. Nobody move. I've got a few things to say to you people."

Tommy saw that Mason was pointing a small silver pistol at Jonetta's back. Mason continued, "Bobby brought Miss Jordan to see me. Unfortunately, it was against her will. I can't imagine why. Only a month ago, she was begging me for an interview."

Jonetta looked at Tommy, her eyes fearful and searching. Why?

Mason held up a Sony Walkman. "I want to play you some interesting tapes." He pressed Play and they heard Jonetta's voice. *Tommy, this is Jonetta. Where have you been? I've called and called. Can you believe they murdered Sonny Boy? You were right all along. I want to help. Please call me as soon as possible.* A three second pause. *Tommy, JJ again. You might be in danger. The feds are moving in on Reed. Please be careful and call me.*

Tommy felt his stomach turn over. Jonetta dropped to one knee. Now, Mason's gun was pointed at her temple.

Mason laughed. "Wait, there's more, gang. Here's a little romance for you." Then they heard Tommy's voice. *Look, I confess. I fell in love with you the first time I saw you. I can't stop thinking about you. Maybe that whole thing about Mason Reed was an excuse to meet you. Even on television, before I met you, I thought you were cute. But, in person, well, you blew me away.*

"Where did you get that?" Tommy demanded.

"Price, you underestimated me. I've had your phones tapped since before I hired you. Unfortunately my worst fears have been confirmed. You're a spy! You and your nigger girlfriend are out to destroy me," Mason almost shouted.

Jonetta collapsed on the floor in a dead faint.

"Pick her up, Bobby, and put her in the limo. Keep a gun on her. She's dangerous." Bobby did as he was told. Mason and Susan descended the steps. "Gentlemen, Susan and I are leaving the country until things settle down. In my absence I need your help." Susan handed Tommy a packet. "In there you'll find a corporate resolution electing you, Thomas Price, the new president of Eagle Records. Congratulations!" Mason said.

"What?" Tommy said.

"Shut up. You're in no position to comment. And you, Mr. Rogers, are the new vice-president. There are also detailed instructions for both of you. By the end of the week, you will shut down Eagle Records, fire everybody, and make sure my money gets out of the country. And to guarantee that you perform your duties to my satisfaction, I'm taking your cohort with me, as security."

"Who? Jonetta?" Tommy asked.

"Yes. Jonetta. Any questions?"

Tommy fell back on the sofa and put his hands to his face.

Gus spoke. "Look, Mr. Reed, I'm an old man. Keep these kids out of it. Let me do your dirty work."

"Sorry, Gus. I need Mr. Price's help. And I know he'll work real hard for me. Right, Tommy? Do your job and save your lover."

"She's not my lover, she's my friend," Tommy protested.

"Whatever, Price. I don't give a damn. I'm taking her with us. You just follow those instructions, to the letter. Now, let's take a ride."

When they reached Lemley Field, Jimmy and the Gulf-stream were ready for takeoff. Tommy's heart ached as Bobby pushed Jonetta up the steps, a gun at her back. If she came to harm, he knew he would never forgive himself. Mason and Susan followed, but at the last moment, Susan broke away and ran to Tommy's side.

"What's this?" Mason shouted over the engines.

"I can't do it. Go without me," Susan shouted back.

"I don't think you'll like prison."

"Mason, just one thing, for me," she said at the top of her voice.

"What, what? Hurry up!"

"Don't let that girl get hurt."

"Suzy, baby, you know how much I like happy endings." Then he closed the door. The rain fell hard on the pitiful trio as the jet took off, turned south, and disappeared.

TWENTY FIVE

On Monday, country music's extended family, including much of its royalty, gathered at the Woodmont Funeral Home to bid Sonny Boy farewell. The eulogy was delivered by Cousin Clyde, a Grand Ole Opry member and Baptist minister. The Pine Top Boys sang a medley of traditional hymns and ended with a stirring rendition of "Amazing Grace." Nary a dry eye remained after Barbara Carr's emotional interpretation of "The Sun Shines in My Sonny Boy's Eyes." A long procession followed the hearse to a bluff overlooking the Harpeth River, where Sonny Boy was laid to rest under a stately oak tree on two hundred acres owned by Ruby. His band members, minus his drummer, served as pall bearers. His grieving, pregnant widow and his famous mother placed roses on his coffin, which had remained closed throughout the proceedings. Despite their best efforts, the Woodmont morticians could not rebuild Sonny Boy's face. Tina earned her mother-in-law's eternal enmity when she left the funeral accompanied by her lover, Jerry Suddath. In Ruby's eyes, Tina was shameless. Even the paternity of the child she carried was uncertain. Mason was conspicuous in his absence, though he had sent a thousand dollars worth of flowers. Ruby was dismayed that Jonetta didn't attend. She needed to talk to her. She had scheduled a meeting with the FBI for Tuesday morning and wanted Jonetta to be there.

Across town, Tommy was nearing the end of a difficult day. He had informed all the employees that "as of immediately" their jobs were terminated. One month's pay and severances ranging from five hundred to five thousand dollars, all specified by Mason, cushioned the blows. Some staffers, the highest paid, did not disguise their outrage. Compounding their anger was the insult of being fired by a *nobody*. To her credit, Susan spent the day at Tommy's side. Tommy was impressed by the firmness she displayed.

One L.A. transplant had wailed, "Terminated? What do you mean, terminated? Who the hell are you to terminate me? I answer to Mason Reed, not some two-bit songwriter."

And Susan had shot back, "Shut up, Les, and sit down. And please, wipe the foam from your mouth. Mason appointed Mr. Price president of Eagle and specifically instructed him to fire you. The whys and wherefores are not your concern. So take your severance, clean out your desk, and vacate the premises. Before five! If you don't like it, get a lawyer."

As Tommy and Susan dealt with agents, executives, accountants, and secretaries, Gus assembled a motley group of songwriters to break the bad news to them.

"Boys, as of today, the House of Reed is history."

One hysterical type shouted, "What? I've got a contract. A two year contract. Man, you can't do this to me!"

"Calm down. I've got some real nice checks here for each of you. We took your weekly draw and multiplied it by five. But you don't get your check unless you sign one of these releases I'm holding." Gus held the stack of papers higher.

The group grumbled but seemed partly mollified. Gus continued, "And here's the best part, guys. We're giving your songs back! Nobody *ever* gets their songs back. Believe me, this is a fair deal. And like they told me to tell you, if you don't like it, get a lawyer."

A slow talking troubadour from Georgia raised his hand.

Gus pointed at him. "Yeah, Billy, say your piece."

"Gus, man, this is crazy. What's really going on?" he drawled.

"Billy, I can't tell you what's really going on. If I did, you wouldn't believe me. I been knocking around this town for thirty years and even I am amazed at what's going on."

"Does it have anything to do with Sonny Boy's murder?" another asked.

"Chuck... no comment." But, by saying nothing, Gus had said a lot, and he knew it. "My advice to you people is simple. Take the money, take your songs, and chalk it up to experience. Welcome to show business."

After firing everyone, Tommy set about the task of asset disposal and money transfers. He wired money from a score of accounts to various overseas banks. He executed countless sell orders for stocks and bonds and then transferred that money. He listed the Crown Tower with Music Row's top real estate agent and instructed her to find a buyer, quickly. He set the asking price ridiculously low, despite the agent's protests. Susan found another agent to handle Mason's Franklin Road estate. Tommy figured Mason's haste was driven by his fear of the government's ability to confiscate property acquired with illegal profits. It was the firesale of the century. Tommy was astounded at the extent of Mason's holdings.

But, whenever he had a spare minute, his thoughts returned to Jonetta. He assumed they had arrived in Colombia at the place Susan called the Ponderosa. The comic quality of its name only amplified the dread Tommy felt. Susan had never been there but Mason had described it to her. She said it would take a battalion of Marines to rescue Jonetta from the quasi-military compound. She described Armadas as "evil but honorable." That didn't make sense to Tommy, and he feared the worst. At three A.M. on Tuesday morning, he awoke from a horrible nightmare about Jonetta. In his dream a pack of ferocious dogs was attacking her as he watched helplessly from the backseat of the limo. His hands and feet were bound with hundreds of guitar strings which cut into his skin. His father came to free him but brought the wrong set of car keys and couldn't unlock the limo. All the while, Tommy could hear the dogs. When he woke up, his shirt was drenched, and he couldn't go back to sleep.

TWENTY SIX

Sunlight flooded the room where Jonetta waited, seated in front of a large, antique desk. She studied an impressive floral arrangement on the table behind the desk and took comfort in the beauty of the flowers. In fact, everything about the room was beautiful. The arched ceiling, the white stuccoed walls, the huge windows through which the warm light poured. Her terror began to dissipate slightly. Surely, in a place so beautiful, no harm could come to her, she told herself.

A woman entered the room. She was tall and her shiny black hair was tied in a bun. She radiated elegance, even though she was dressed for tennis. In one hand she held a tennis racket, in the other, a Bible. Jonetta looked at her intently. The woman sat in the chair behind the desk and smiled.

"Good morning, señorita. Did you sleep well?" she asked in a halting but kindly manner.

Jonetta shook her head, no.

"I'm sorry. I can arrange for sleeping... ah, how would you say it? Medications?"

"No. I won't take any pills."

"I understand. Maybe a massage would help. I can send my masseuse to your room tonight, before you retire. She's excellent. Trained in Sweden."

"Thank you. Perhaps. But may I ask, who are you?"

"Pardon me for not introducing myself. I am Elena Armadas. My husband is Hector Armadas."

Upon hearing his name, tears filled Jonetta's eyes. Elena reached inside her desk for tissues and gave one to Jonetta. She dabbed her eyes and regained her composure.

Elena continued. "I'm sorry, I know this must be very hard for you. I can't imagine what you are feeling. My husband is very upset that you were brought here. He is angry with Señor Reed. But, of course, they are business partners, and in business, differences arise. Hector asked me to meet with you to reassure you. He is assessing your situation, and he is confident that in time you can be returned to your home. He doesn't want you to be frightened."

"Thank you, Mrs. Armadas, thank you."

"Please call me Elena. How may I address you?"

"Jonetta."

"Jonetta. I've never heard that name. It's pretty, almost Spanish. Is it a common name for American girls?"

"No, it's rare, like me," Jonetta said, repeating a line her mother had told her a thousand times. "I was named for my father, Joe."

"Does he know you're here?"

"No, he's dead. But my mother..." Again, tears filled her eyes and she couldn't speak.

"Yes, your mother? Tell me."

"My mother has a heart condition. I'm her only child. When she finds out... well, I'm very concerned about her."

Elena looked down for a moment. "Perhaps I can arrange for you to telephone your mother. I can't promise that, but I will try."

Jonetta leaned forward, "Thank you, Elena. That would help if I could talk to her. I usually call her every night." She hesitated and then asked "Has your husband told you what he plans to do with me?"

"No!" Elena said firmly. Anger flashed across her brown

eyes. Then, she softened her tone. "I learned long ago not to concern myself with Hector's business. In my country, a woman's work is her home, her family. But we are in an unusual situation here. You are *in* my home, an uninvited guest anxious to leave. I have sympathy for you, but my influence is limited. But, as long as you are here, I will do my best to make you comfortable and... safe." She handed Jonetta the Bible. "This Bible is in English. Perhaps you will find it a source of comfort."

Jonetta took the Bible and held it firmly. "Thank you, Elena. Thank you for your kindness toward me."

"Tonight, your attendance is requested at a banquet."

"But..."

"Señorita, you have no choice. Every week we host a formal dinner and everyone is expected to attend. My assistant, Lucinda, will provide a wardrobe for you."

As if on cue, Lucinda entered the room. She was maybe nineteen, pretty, stylish, and she seemed a little bashful, as if embarrassed by the circumstances. Elena continued, "Tell Lucinda your sizes. She will also show you around. As long as you are with her, you may do as you like. But don't even consider attempting to leave La Ponderosa. The entire estate is surrounded by an eight foot electric fence and is patrolled by dogs and *sicarios*."

"*Sicarios?*"

"Yes. These are young men my husband employs to assist him in his business. But they are even more vicious than the dogs. Avoid them at all costs. I believe you can survive this ordeal if you follow some advice in that holy book you hold."

"Yes, tell me."

"Try to be as gentle as a dove and as wise as a serpent." Elena rose. "And now I must leave you. I'm late for tennis. Is there anything else?"

"My mother..."

"I said I would try. Be careful and may God bless you."

Jonetta wanted to follow her, sensing safety in her presence. For the first time since that fat pig Bobby forced her into his car, she felt hopeful.

◆

The arrival of the kidnapped American beauty was the talk of La Ponderosa. One person in particular took an interest in her. Ed Green had acquired a sexual preference for black women during his service as a young man to Idi Amin, who had supplied the mercenary with Uganda's most desirable women. Because of Green's dangerous perversions, a dozen Ugandan beauties had disappeared. Green thought Jonetta was the most exciting woman he had ever seen. He couldn't wait.

TWENTY SEVEN

Within an hour after their meeting with Ruby and Mavis, Special Agents Doyle Masters and J.W. Faust entered the lobby of Eagle Records carrying a search warrant. But, the place was empty. They explored the entire floor and found only deserted offices. No people, no papers, nothing but scattered furniture and assorted trash.

"What do you think?"

"Don't know. I guess somebody tipped 'em off. They sure left in a hurry."

"Be quiet. Somebody's coming." The agents drew their pistols as they heard someone fumble with the door knob to the conference room. An elderly white man in a uniform entered, saw the agents, dropped his broom, and threw up his hands.

"Don't shoot mister!" he cried.

"Who are you?"

"Rufus Upshaw, the janitor. I ain't done nothing and I don't have nothing."

The agents lowered their weapons. "Relax, Mr. Upshaw. Nobody's going to hurt you. I'm Agent Faust, FBI. This is Agent Masters. Where is everybody?"

"FBI?"

"Yes sir. Doyle, show him your badge. Mr. Upshaw, you can lower your hands now. We have a warrant to search this place, but there's not much left to search. Like I said, where is everybody?"

"Gone. Flew the coop."

"We can see that. When did it happen?"

"Yesterday. They all got fired."

"Who fired them?"

"Don't know his name. Young fella. It wasn't Mr. Reed."

"Are you referring to Mason Reed?"

"Yes sir. I haven't seen him in a while. Are you going to read me my rights?"

"Have you done anything wrong?"

"No sir. Not one thing."

"And we're not accusing you of anything, sir. We're just investigating. If you could help us, we'd be much obliged."

"Well, I guess you want to know who killed Sonny Boy. Right?"

"That's a good start. Do you know?"

"Yes sir. The black moozlims. They did it, trying to start a race war. They're gonna kill all the country music stars if they have to. You boys better keep an eye on 'em. Say, did you boys know Mr. Hoover?"

"No sir, never knew the man," Faust said and chuckled. They began to leave when Rufus reached in his pocket for a piece of paper.

"Here, Mr. G-man, this might help you. The fella what did all the firing gave me this phone number to call if I had any problems."

"Let me see that," Masters said and copied the number. "Now that's more like it, Rufus. Thanks for your help."

"Yes sir. But watch out for them moozlims. I'm warning ya."

Within minutes the agents had traced the phone number. Within an hour, they had obtained a search warrant for Tommy's apartment. They confiscated his recorded messages, a few files pertaining to the House of Reed, a roach clip, and six marijuana seeds they found in an ashtray. In addition to his other problems, Tommy was now facing federal drug charges.

TWENTY EIGHT

In the grand dining room uniformed waiters served the first course, a cold curried asparagus soup. The flags of all of the South American countries hung from the twenty-foot ceiling. An elaborate cut glass chandelier sprayed soft light on the diners, who were dressed in formal evening wear. Hector sat at one end of the table, Elena at the other. Elena was regal in a sleek blue silk gown that fell off her shoulders. Hector was the picture of authority, a man firmly in control of his environment.

Wearing an Oscar de la Renta original, which Elena had provided, Jonetta was seated between a bald headed man with badly pocked skin and thick eyebrows, and a blonde, very handsome man who spoke with a pronounced German accent. Mason was seated across from her. He seemed subdued, almost sad. Jonetta, ever the journalist, studied all the people at the table. She guessed the couple closest to Hector to be family. She was right. It was Carlos and his wife, Maria. Jonetta's guardian, Lucinda, was also present, seated next to Jimmy, Mason's pilot. Fat Bobby must be dining with the help, she thought, noting his absence.

Hector rose and held up a glass of champagne. "Tonight, in deference to our American guests, we will speak English, as much as possible. As we all know, because of music, movies, and all the other great American entertainments, English will soon become the universal language. But, Spanish will be a close second! To the good old U.S.A.!"

To the U.S.A., the crowd responded. Jonetta raised her glass but didn't drink.

"Don't you like champagne? This is the finest, Dom Perignon," the man with bad skin asked her. He spoke with a flat, midwestern twang.

"No thank you. My stomach's upset. I don't have an appetite."

"But the champagne will settle your stomach and stimulate your appetite," he said soothingly. "It's not poison, I promise."

She gingerly sipped the champagne. The small amount she ingested pleasantly warmed her empty stomach. She took another, larger sip. Then she sampled the soup, which was delicious.

The man introduced himself as Ed Green, a fellow American. He said he was head of security for La Ponderosa.

"I make sure only the invited enter La Ponderosa and only the excused leave."

The blonde introduced himself as Gunther Beck. He explained that he managed the stables.

"Do you ride, Miss Jordan?" Gunther asked her.

"No, I never learned."

"Vould you like to?"

"I don't think that would be permitted."

"Perhaps I can arrange a riding lesson."

"Yes, that would be nice." Jonetta engaged in small talk as if on automatic pilot. The unreality of the situation was bizarre, otherworldly. All about her she saw smiling faces, yet she knew she was in mortal danger. She didn't know how long she could maintain her composure. She wanted to stand and scream, but, of course, she didn't.

Mason rose to offer his response to Hector's toast. "My dear friends, I want to salute our host, our patron, Don Hector. Despite the awkward and unexpected nature of my party's arrival here, we have been graciously welcomed by Don Hector and his lovely wife, Elena. I thank you, Don Hector, and I apologize for any inconvenience we have caused you, your family, or your staff. We are grateful that you have taken us in during these difficult times. Here's to you, Hector Armadas Galéna, long may you live and prosper!"

Hear, hear! Bravo! The crowd called out enthusiastically.

Gunther jumped up and executed a stiff armed salute and shouted, *"Seig heil!"* Jonetta couldn't believe what she was seeing and hearing.

Green leaned over her and grabbed the German. "Cut out that Nazi bullshit, asshole!"

Gunther looked at Green with fierce, blue eyes and spat, *"Verpiss Dich!"* The men began to wrestle with each other as Jonetta cowered beneath them.

"Gentlemen, control yourselves!" Hector ordered. The men sat down, straightened their tuxedos and shot killing looks at each other.

"It seems like you've got your hands full, Miss Jordan. You have excited their animal spirits. Be careful," Mason said through a sinister smile.

Dinner proceeded quietly until, as dessert was being served, a brightly costumed figure ran into the room and executed double handsprings. He wore a mask, tights and a pointed hat.

"The jester is here! All hail the jester!" Hector shouted with childlike glee.

The jester bowed low to Hector.

> *I am here at the faithful service*
> *Of the mighty Don Hector Armadas*

"Thank you, jester. You may go to work."

The jester addressed the group.

> *There are strangers among us*
> *Who do not speak Spanish*
> *So tonight I will furnish*
> *My jesting in English*

The table applauded him.

> *Please accept my endeavors*
> *To be witty and clever*
> *In a language I fear*
> *More suited to . . . Shakespeare*

The jester approached Elena. He knelt before her and took her hand.

> *Beautiful lady, forsake old man Hector*
> *And dare to love me, the dashing young jester*

Elena shook her head and laughed, "No! No!" She was enjoying herself.

> *I can love you much better*
> *Much sweeter, much longer,*
> *I may be the fool*
> *But my love is much stronger*

"No. Never!" Elena had heard this routine before. The jester always flirted with her.

> *But why, why, why,*
> *Why are you so loyal*
> *(he pointed to Hector)*
> *To an ass, so royal?*

Hector laughed and shouted, "Watch out, jester! Remember who feeds you."

The jester eyed the other diners, setting his sights on Carlos, who wasn't smiling.

Why are you so gloomy, Don Carlos?
Has the king's brother suffered a loss?

"No, jester. I ate too fast. I have indigestion," Carlos replied in Spanish, patting his stomach.

Oh, you suffer now from gases
But we suffer later . . . when it passes!

The jester made a really loud, obnoxious farting noise, held his nose, and ran to the other end of the room. Even Jonetta giggled at the antics of the court clown. To her chagrin, he caught her eye and sauntered toward her. He carefully examined the nervous young woman. He held up her left arm.

I see by your left hand
You've met the right man

Jonetta smiled and raised her hand higher, showing off her very respectable diamond engagement ring. She wanted them to know that someone back home cared about her. The jester continued.

According to gossip
You have been kidnapped

"Yes, sir. I was kidnapped," Jonetta replied in a strong, clear voice. The mood in the room instantly darkened. The jester whispered loudly:

I could tell you an earful
But it might make you fearful!

146

Hector jumped up. "Jester, watch your step!" he said in Spanish. "I pay you to be funny." The jester threw up his hands in protest.

Sometimes my humor
Makes you mad, Don Hector
But that is the nature
Of my work as a jester
What others fear tell you
You know that I do.

"Proceed with caution," Hector said. The jester stood ramrod straight and pointed his finger at Hector.

Your riches are vast
Your power is great
But it will not last
If you make this mistake

Then, the jester pointed at Jonetta.

Es verdad, mis amigos
This girl must return
Or the House of Armadas
Will burn, burn, burn!

The jester cartwheeled from the room. Jonetta felt as if she had witnessed a miracle. That man may have saved my life, she thought. Was he an angel?

TWENTY NINE

The telephone was placed by Susan on the floor in the center of the circle surrounded by the sofa where the three of them sat, waiting for the call Mason had promised to make between three and five P.M., Nashville time. After the kidnapping, Gus and Tommy had moved into Mason's home, at Susan's urging. Eight thousand square feet provided plenty of space to spread out in, but they gravitated to each other, bound together by common peril. Last night, Tommy had shared Susan's bed. There was no sex; they simply held each other. And despite the gravity of the situation, Gus was rather enjoying his fling with luxury. He languished in Mason's steam room, soaked in his jacuzzi, and slept soundly in his oversized bed, between satin sheets.

But now, they waited.

"He did say between three and five?" Tommy asked nervously.

"Right," Susan answered.

"Will he call, like he promised?"

"I think so, Tommy. There's a lot at stake for him, too. Try to relax. You're making me jumpy."

"When he calls, you'll confirm that we did everything he wanted?"

"Yes, of course."

"I hope he still trusts you. Do you think they'll fly her back tomorrow? And where to? And how? A commercial airline?"

"Look, sit down. Quit pacing around. How do I know anything? We did the best we could. That's all we can do."

The clock read 3:20. Gus stood up. "Hey, how 'bout I get my guitar? Might help pass the time."

Tommy frowned, but Susan said, "Sure. Sounds like a good idea."

Gus returned with his Martin. He tuned it to the grand piano, returned to the sofa, and played softly.

"That's nice, what is it?" Susan asked.

"A new song I'm writing."

"Has it got any words?"

"Ain't finished. Takes a while to get 'em right. My motto is, We serve no rhyme before its time."

"Why don't you play me one that is finished?" Susan stretched out on the floor, ready to be entertained.

"Sure, missy. I love serenading the ladies." He chose an old song, one the girls always liked. Tommy's initial annoyance melted away as Gus sang about unrequited love.

"Oh, Gus, I loved it!" Susan exclaimed. "I didn't realize you were such a . . . "

"Great singer?" Gus asked sarcastically. He knew he was a merely adequate singer.

"I *like* your voice. It has character. But I was going to say I didn't realize you're such a poet."

"I've been trying to tell everybody about this guy," Tommy said. "He *is* a poet."

"Please play another one. Please," Susan begged sweetly. Gus obliged and played a powerful song about losing innocence, and in the process, finding faith. It struck Susan like a revelation.

"Wow." She wiped a tear from her cheek. "That hit close to home. I was really moved. Thank you, Gus. Thank you for writing that song."

Gus smiled, blushing. "Thank you, Susan, for liking it. Now it's Tommy's turn to play one. Take it, kid." Gus held out his guitar. Tommy took it somewhat reluctantly. He fumbled over a few unrelated chords as he searched his mind. He chose one close to his heart, a song inspired by his mother's death.

After he had finished, the room was silent for a moment. "Great song, kid," Gus whispered and patted him on the shoulder.

Susan sprang to her feet. "It just hit me. *This* is what it's all about. It's not about the money, the charts, the gold records, the awards, the glamour, the glitz. Those things are what's wrong with this business. What's right about it are moments like this. Moments when the truth is shared among friends."

"Amen, sister. Testify!" Gus laughed and slapped his knee.

"I'm serious. I just had an insight. I see it clearly now. Maybe you guys have known it all along. But I've never experienced it, and it feels wonderful!" Susan twirled around like a child on a playground.

"Missy, you're right, this is what it's all about. The songs get lost in the scramble. And the truth is in the songs." Gus lit a smoke and reflected, "When I first came to Nashville we had guitar pulls like this all the time. Hell, that's how we pitched our songs, before all the middlemen showed up. We'd sit in a circle with other writers, record producers, maybe a star or two, and swap songs all night long. Then country music got to be a big bucks affair, and it changed. Money changes everything it touches. Nowadays writers won't even share their songs with each other. And why? They're afraid somebody will rip off a great line or steal a catchy title." Gus blew a perfect smoke ring, then put his finger through it and erased it. "In the modern country music business, they emphasize the business, not the music. And what happens? The music suffers. And the truth is hidden a little more, for a little while longer. Yeah, this town changed. And not for the better."

"I wish I could have seen it then," Tommy said wistfully.

"Come on guys. Don't give up. It can change back. I've got an idea!" Susan said brightly.

"What's that, little lady?" Gus asked.

"Let's start our own record company!" She held her hands up and waited for their response.

Tommy said, "Susan, we just destroyed a record company. Now you want to start another one? Get real." Tommy refused to get caught up in Susan's fantasy, not even to pass the time.

"I mean the right kind of record company. One that's dedicated to truth, to art ... to the songs."

"Cut the crap, Susan." Tommy was angry. "You and Mason blow into town, spread your dirty money around, play games with people's lives, and now, you think you can snap your fingers and change all that. One person has been murdered, one has been kidnapped and may be murdered, and you want to talk about art and truth. Gimme a break."

"Lighten up, Tommy," Gus said. "We're all under a lot of pressure. She was only ..."

Susan cut him off. "That's okay, Gus. Tommy's right. Who am I to talk about these things?" Her shoulders dropped from the weight of her shame. "I'm a Hollywood whore who couldn't make it as an actress. I had my shot at art, and I failed. I failed badly. Instead, I raised lying to an art form. I don't deserve a second chance. I've already had a hundred second chances in my life. Every time, I made the wrong choice."

Tommy's anger, once expressed, disappeared. His heart went out to Susan. "That's not right," he said. He knew he had really hurt Susan. "You chose to stay and help us free Jonetta. That took a lot of courage. You could have gone to Colombia, but you didn't. You've been great the last couple of days. Without you, I would have been lost. I'm sorry I dumped on you."

The telephone rang. They jumped, startled by its rude report. Susan picked up the receiver.

"Hello. Mason? Yeah, you sound like you're next door. I can't believe you're calling from South America. How are you? Good. How was the flight down? Good. Is the girl all right? Yeah. Look, we've done everything you wanted. Tommy and Gus have been great. I think you'll be pleased. An agent is supposed to come this afternoon to look at the house. Yeah. Yeah. No, the press hasn't picked up on anything yet. Believe me, it's coming. Right. Sure. Okay. Yeah, he's right here. I'll put him on." Susan held the phone out. "He wants to talk to you."

"Me?" Tommy asked.

"Yes, you. Take it."

"Mr. Reed. Yes sir. Right. Fine. Good. We've done everything on the list. It went okay. Only three threatened to sue. Right. Of course. So, how is Jonetta? Yes sir. She played tennis yesterday? That sounds good. Mr. Reed, we've held up our end of the bargain, I hope ... I'm not trying to pressure you. How can I? You hold all the cards. Just remember Jonetta is a local celebrity. I'm sure they're looking for her now. She called her mother? And the station? Did they buy it? Right, but that's a temporary ..."

Tommy turned around. "He said someone wants to talk to me. Maybe he'll put Jonetta on." After a few interminable moments, Tommy heard another voice. "Hello, yes, this is Mr. Price. Who is this?" Tommy's jaw dropped. It was Armadas. "Mr. Armadas? Yes sir. Right. Yes, Miss Jordan is my friend. I'm very concerned about her. Yes sir. I'm sure you will, but... we need to get her back, as soon as possible, before the press gets hold of this. Right. Yes sir. I'm listening." Tommy nodded his head as Hector talked at length. "I really don't think that's possible, Mr. Armadas. They will never go for that. I see. Right. Yes sir, I understand. I understand completely. Yes sir. Goodbye."

Tommy hung up the phone and fell back on the sofa. His face was drained of color, his eyes unfocused.

"Well?" Susan asked. "Was that Armadas?"

"Yeah. The one and only."

"Damn, Tommy, what did the man say?" Gus asked.

"He said that before he'll return Jonetta, he wants five minutes on the CMA awards show next month."

"What? Why?"

"He wants to address the nation, as he put it."

"That's crazy," Gus huffed. "It'll never happen."

"Does he intend to come to Nashville?" Susan asked.

"No. He wants to do a satellite feed. He said he could pull it off."

"And if he doesn't get the five minutes?"

"He'll kill her. He promised to do it quickly, so she wouldn't suffer. But, he said he *would* execute her."

"Is that all?"

"No. He said he was sorry about Sonny Boy. He said he was his biggest fan. Said Sonny Boy chose his fate. Something about lead or silver. He also said 'Wayward Angel' was the best song Sonny Boy McDaniel had ever released. He predicted a number one." Tommy looked at Gus and shook his head in disbelief.

"I'll be goddamned," Gus whispered.

The doorbell rang. "That must be the real estate agent," Susan said. "I'll get it." She returned with two men in business suits.

"Are you agents?" Tommy asked.

"Yes, we are. Are you Thomas Price?" one of them asked.

"Tommy, these guys don't sell real estate. They're from the FBI," Susan said.

"Perfect, just perfect." Tommy sighed. He decided right then and there to cooperate. "It's about time you guys got involved. I think we need your help."

Agent Faust smiled. "That's what we're here for. You help us. We help you. Everything works out better that way. But I've got to tell you, Mr. Price, we're considering charges against you."

"Like what? I haven't done anything."

Faust held up a plastic baggy containing the marijuana seeds. "A controlled substance violation to start with. And, of course, there's the whole Eagle mess. And the murder of Sonny Boy McDaniel. And your connection with Mason Reed, and, of course, Hector Armadas. We're very interested in Mr. Armadas."

"You can add one kidnapping to that list," Tommy said.

"A kidnapping? What are you talking about?" Masters asked.

"Mason Reed kidnapped Jonetta Jordan, the TV reporter, and took her to Colombia," Tommy said.

"My God! This thing's out of control," Faust said. "It *is* a good thing we showed up."

Tommy swallowed hard. "I want to cooperate. But, I better get a lawyer."

"That's your right, Mr. Price. There's the phone. Start calling."

Tommy called his father, but he wasn't in his office. Then he thought of Charles Robinson, Jonetta's fiancé. Certainly, Charles would help.

THIRTY

The lights of Nashville sparkled and spread out as far as Tommy could see. He was standing in Charles Robinson's impressive law office on the twenty-eighth floor of the Standard Life Building. Three miles away the Crown Tower was clearly visible, anchoring Music Row. He could see that the first ten floors of the Tower were illuminated, filled with people working late. He wondered about the people in those offices. What were they doing? What dreams led them on? What desires? The top two floors of the Crown Tower were dark and empty, and of course, he knew why. The irony of it all made him smile.

"A penny for your thoughts?" Gus asked him.

"I can see the Crown Tower from here. All the floors are lit up, all except ours. It's seven-thirty on a Wednesday night. Those people oughta go home to their families. They oughta get out of there!"

"Maybe they don't have families to go home to. Have you thought about that? Maybe that's why they work late," Susan said knowingly.

Tommy said, "Yeah, you're right. Not too long ago I was down there with 'em, burning my share of electricity. Happy to be working late."

The door flew open. Two men entered. One was Charles Robinson, a tall, elegant man in his early thirties. He was wearing a dark brown three piece suit, high gloss power shoes, and a hand painted tie. He could have stepped from the pages of *GQ* magazine. The other was Jeff Frazier, a

155

partner at Barkley and Stokes who specialized in criminal defense. He was lean and somewhat disheveled, with longish brown hair and a theatrical handlebar moustache.

Frazier spoke hurriedly, "Okay gang, here's the deal. The feds realize you people are not dangerous criminals."

"That's good," Tommy said.

"Right, that *is* good. But it's not that simple. Let me go over each situation, case by case."

"Fire away," Gus said.

"Gus, you're in pretty good shape. As long as you cooperate, and nothing else turns up, then I think you can relax."

Gus smiled. "Thanks, counselor."

"As for you, Susan. They're looking at you harder because of your long and close association with Reed. By the same token, you're more valuable to them. You could be a big help to these guys. You understand Reed and, I assume, you know something about the Armadas connection."

"Mason never told me much about Armadas," Susan said. "And I was smart enough not to ask a lot of questions."

"Well, that may be the case, but, still, I'm afraid you're in some pretty serious trouble. You'll need to get your own lawyer, and a good one. We can't represent all three of you. Conflicts of interest will certainly arise as this thing develops."

"The only lawyers I know are show biz dealmakers. And they're in L.A.," Susan said.

Charles reassured her, "We'll help you find somebody, if it comes to that. Try not to worry."

"Tommy." Frazier continued, turning to face him.

"Yes sir. I'm all ears."

"I don't think they'll press the drug charge, although they could."

"Six measly seeds?"

"I know, it's ridiculous. But, they will use the threat of prosecution as leverage. Your role in transferring monies is more serious. But, I think we can convince them you were acting under duress..."

"That's an understatement," Tommy said.

"The bottom line for all of you is this: if you cooperate fully, and if we have a good result, everybody walks. But, I say that based on what I know now. If you haven't told me everything..."

Tommy interrupted Frazier. "What do you mean by a good result?"

"If you help build the case against Reed and they obtain a conviction, that's a good result. Whatever you can do in regard to Armadas is most helpful. He's the ultimate target. And..." Frazier hesitated.

"And what?" Tommy asked.

"If we get Jonetta back safely. That's very important."

"But we all want that! What do you think we've been doing for the last three days? We've been trying our damnedest to get Jonetta back." Tommy was agitated, tired, and approaching an emotional meltdown. Charles walked over to him and put his hand on Tommy's shoulder.

"Nobody wants her back more than I do. What Jeff is trying to say is this: If something happens to Jonetta, God forbid, then the pressure increases on the feds to..."

"To what? Blame somebody? Is that what you're getting at? Don't tell me they'll come after us," Tommy said excitedly.

"Kidnapping is a very serious federal crime," Frazier said. "If something happens to Jonetta, the FBI is going to look very closely at the role each of you played in the kidnapping, even if your role was involuntary."

Tommy felt like he was trapped in a nightmare designed

by Kafka. He spoke quietly, with determination, "Well, what are we waiting for? We should be talking about how to get Jonetta back."

"You're right. Are all of you ready to cooperate fully?" Frazier asked. *Yes*, they said in unison.

"Susan, you too? That is, after we get you a good lawyer."

"Yes, of course."

"All right. Now let's go to the conference room, one by one, and get to work. You first, Tommy. Faust and Masters are waiting. Let me warn you that the DEA has arrived. A guy named Jamison, I believe. He seems to have his own agenda."

For the next five hours Tommy and Gus were interrogated individually by Faust, Masters, and DEA agent Al Jamison. With few exceptions, they answered each question honestly and completely. Pizzas, colas, cigarettes and coffee helped maintain their stamina and sustain the pace. By midnight, however, everyone was exhausted, operating on reserve nervous energy.

Jamison startled the assembled group when he announced, "Tomorrow, I'm going to recommend to Washington that we invade the Ponderosa and rescue the girl. Armadas has finally given us the excuse we've needed to blow him away. I think the Colombian government would support us."

"Al, forget the John Wayne approach, okay? If you go in there with guns blazing, the girl dies. You know that," Faust argued.

"Let me remind you, Mr. Jamison, that's my fiancée we're talking about," Charles added, one degree shy of angry.

Jamison looked at Charles. "Mr. Robinson, it's time you faced reality."

"What reality?" Charles demanded, clenching his fist.

"Tell him, Doyle. Tell him the truth about kidnappers," Jamison said.

Masters stood up. "There's a good chance Jonetta is already dead," he said with resignation.

"But she spoke with her mother yesterday and she was fine," Charles said, his voice full of desperate hope. Throughout the ordeal, Tommy had been mightily impressed by Charles' poise under pressure. He could definitely see why Jonetta had decided to marry the man. But Charles, too, was reaching the breaking point.

"That's right. Yesterday she spoke to her mother, and to the television station. Those are good signs," Faust said firmly. "Just remember, Patty Hearst survived. We're working on the assumption she's alive. We have to." Faust rubbed his face with his hands trying to dispel the fatigue. He looked at his wristwatch. "It's almost one A.M. Let's wrap it up. Tomorrow, Doyle and I will notify the press. It's important that we control the media process as much as possible. To help us do that, none of you should speak to anyone with the media. That includes you, Al."

Jamison grunted his reluctant assent. Faust pointed to Tommy, Gus, and Susan. "You three are now under federal protective custody. I assume Hector's henchmen have already arrived in Nashville. If not, they're on their way. You can stay out on Franklin Road, where we picked you up. That place seemed well secured. We'll make Reed's home our command central. There will be several agents with you at all times. Don't try anything stupid. Let's meet there at nine o'clock in the morning. At that time, we'll begin implementation of the next step."

"Which is?" Charles asked.

"I guess we're going to ask the CMA to give us five minutes on their awards show. That is the ransom, as I understand it. Right, Mr. Price?" Faust asked.

"That's right," Tommy said wearily. Jamison threw an empty cola in the garbage can as if to make a point, but he remained silent, too tired to debate.

"Okay. Anything else?" Faust looked around the room.

"What about Jonetta's mother?" Charles said.

"Good point," Faust replied. "We better put somebody with her. Charles, try to prepare Mrs. Jordan for the approaching shit storm, excuse my choice of words." Charles glumly nodded his head.

"Okay, that's it for tonight. Try to get some sleep. You're gonna need it," Faust concluded

They heard a soft knock on the door. Tommy's father stuck his head inside.

"Price?"

"Dad! My God, how did you get here so fast?'

"I left as soon as I got your message. I was in New York so I went straight to LaGuardia. Can you spare a toothbrush?" He smiled and stretched out his arms.

Tommy jumped up, ran to his father, and hugged him tightly for a long time.

THIRTY ONE

As Ethel waited for six o'clock she mentally recited the twenty third psalm. *The Lord is my shepherd. I shall not want. He maketh me...* Over and over she repeated the lines from memory. The hallowed words almost crowded out the worry, fear, and panic which threatened to overwhelm her mind. Not since Big Joe's heart attack, when she was alone in the hospital waiting room, had her faith been tested so directly. When the doctor had appeared and had shaken his head, she knew he was gone. Despite all her prayers, pleadings, and promises, the Lord took Joe, just when she needed him most. Would, could God take her precious Jonetta? *Though I walk through the valley of the shadow of death...*

"Mrs. Jordan."

Ethel continued rocking gently back and forth, oblivious to the stranger standing behind her.

"Mrs. Jordan."

"Yes?"

"The doctor prescribed some pills to calm you down. Why don't you take one?"

Ethel turned slightly to face her intruder. She saw a smiling black woman dressed in a plain, dark suit, holding a glass of water and offering a small white pill.

"I didn't know the FBI hired black women," Ethel said suspiciously.

"They don't hire many, but they hired me. Now why don't you take this pill the doctor prescribed?"

"Where did you grow up?" Ethel asked.

"Birmingham."

"I've got a baby sister in Huntsville."

"Well, that's right down the road. Would you like to have her come up and keep you company?"

"Heavens no, child! We get all over each other's nerves. When I called her this morning she went hysterical on me. I love my sister but she'd only be a burden."

"Mrs. Jordan, how 'bout this pill?"

"Honey, instead of that pill, bring me that bottle of Mogen David that's on top the 'frigerator. A glass or two will settle me down nicely. I don't like taking pills. Only Bufferin for my knees."

On the television, the local evening news began. The lead story was, of course, Jonetta's kidnapping. The five-thirty national news had contained a brief mention of the event, but the Nashville news hour would be dominated by the story. CNN was also covering the kidnapping, but Ethel couldn't afford cable.

The city was shocked to learn today that Channel Six's own Jonetta Jordan was kidnapped at gunpoint by music business mogul Mason Reed and flown to South America, where she is being held at the estate of Colombian drug lord Hector Armadas. According to information released by the FBI, the crime occurred last Sunday afternoon in Nashville and is related to Miss Jordan's investigation of the recent murder of country music star Sonny Boy McDaniel. Apparently Miss Jordan had uncovered a link between McDaniel's murder, Mason Reed, and the powerful Armadas, one of the richest men in the world.

Music Row was in a state of disbelief at the amazing involvement of industry heavyweight Reed, who, within months of relocating in Nashville from California, had launched a successful record label and produced a major motion picture, which had been scheduled for a Christmas release. Coming on the heels of the sensational murder of Sonny Boy McDaniel, the kidnapping of Miss Jordan has normally unflappable music business observers searching for adjectives to describe the incredible chain of events.

Later tonight, at eight P.M., Channel Six will present a special one hour show devoted to this story. We'll take a closer look at the career and life of Jonetta Jordan, one of Nashville's favorite personalities. We'll also examine Mason Reed and attempt to find an explanation for his bizarre behavior. Our staff has prepared a profile of cocaine baron Hector Armadas, who, it appears, is the force behind these tragedies. And we have an interview with country music great, Ruby McDaniel, mother of the slain recording star. Before we turn to other news, let us extend our prayers and sympathy to Jonetta, her family, and friends. Jonetta's Channel Six family will be with you every step of the way until her safe return. And now, for these commercial messages.

Agent Alice Tilden sat down beside Ethel and took her hand. "Mrs. Jordan, I promise you, we're going to do everything we can to bring Jonetta home safely."

Ethel didn't reply. She resumed her slow rocking and silent recitations, placing her hopes squarely with heaven, not the FBI.

THIRTY TWO

If I get out of this place alive I'm going to buy and board a horse, Jonetta promised herself. Jonetta's mount, Loretta Lynn, was an older, black mare, content to follow the other horses along the trails which wound through La Ponderosa. Gunther and Lucinda rode ahead. Behind her, ominously, was an unsmiling guard with a rifle. She knew there was no possibility of escape. Her horse was too slow, and she assumed the guard was a good shot. If she did escape the Ponderosa, where would she go? Into the jungle, to be hunted by dogs? No. Her only hope of returning home was being released. Even if the Marines appeared on the horizon in wave after wave of helicopters, she knew she would die. She hated to admit it, but her fate was in the hands of a mixed-up country songwriter from New Jersey.

Jonetta maintained her sanity during the long days and nights by keeping a journal and reading the Bible Elena had given her. With the exception of one daily activity such as tennis, horseback riding or walking, she spent all her time locked in her room. She never watched television, read a newspaper or magazine, nor spoke with anyone other than Lucinda, who was pleasant but limited company. Lucinda's interests seemed restricted to fashion, boys, and American pop culture. To Lucinda, America was a golden land, peopled exclusively by millionaires and movie stars. Jonetta tried to disabuse her of these false notions, but to no avail. Lucinda was young, superficial, and determined to preserve her fantasies, preferring them to less attractive realities. By observing and talking with Lucinda, Jonetta perceived for the first time the insidious effects of glamour. Jonetta saw much of herself in Lucinda, and she resolved to become a more serious, thoughtful person, if she got the chance.

Gunther raised his hand, signaling the group to halt. Suddenly, from out of the tangled growth, a group of men on foot surrounded them. They were dressed in makeshift uniforms and carried submachine guns. Jonetta knew instinctively they were the dreaded *sicarios*. She counted nine men, none older than twenty-five. They eyed her closely and their stares frightened her. One walked up to her, leering, and ran his hand down her leg.

The leader of the gang and Gunther engaged in a tense exchange, gesticulating and speaking loudly in Spanish. Her terror was magnified by her inability to understand the conversation. The *sicario* pointed at her several times as he waved his arms. Jonetta asked Lucinda what was happening.

"The *sicario* told Gunther he had instructions to take you back for interrogation," Lucinda explained. "But Gunther said he knows of no such instructions and that you were in his custody and he wouldn't allow it. The *sicario* said Colonel Green issued the order and that Green is head of security and his word is final in these matters."

Fear shot through Jonetta's nervous system, tensing every muscle in her body. The argument between the *sicario* and Gunther grew more heated.

"What are they saying now?" Jonetta whispered.

"The *sicario* said we are trespassing on their territory. He said he has the right to shoot trespassers. No questions asked. Gunther said the land belongs to Armadas and he has Hector's permission to ride anywhere in La Ponderosa."

Gunther then pulled a silver Luger and pointed it at the *sicario*'s face. The *sicario* backed away and spat at Gunther's feet. He motioned to his men to disband.

"You will answer to Colonel Green for this," the leader shouted. "God help you!"

Then, as quickly as they had appeared, they were gone, dissolving into the chaparral like apparitions.

After this incident Jonetta was confined to her room and the grounds within one hundred yards of her room. She had no desire to venture further.

THIRTY THREE

As Mason had promised, *in writing*, on October 2, 1992, Sonny Boy McDaniel's recording of "Wayward Angel" reached the number one position on *Billboard's* country music chart. The record was also at number thirty-seven with a bullet on the pop charts, making it a rare "crossover" hit.

For Ruby, her son's posthumous achievement was bittersweet. Choking back emotions so strong they threatened to overwhelm her, she hung the *Billboard* chart next to her favorite portrait of Sonny Boy, a charcoal drawing done on his twenty-first birthday. Finally, her boy was on top. She only hoped that, wherever he was, he knew he had made it to number one.

Thirty Four

By using her considerable clout and goodwill, Ruby persuaded a reluctant CMA director, Irene Randall, to call an emergency meeting of the board of directors to consider the FBI's extraordinary request. It would be a tough sell. The live, televised CMA awards show was country music's biggest night of the year, reaching a huge audience. The board would be loathe to tamper with its crown jewel.

Tommy waited nervously with his father and Charles in the spacious lobby of the CMA headquarters. For the first time since his grandfather's funeral Tommy was wearing a suit and a tie. His hair was neatly trimmed, shorter than it had been in years. He was determined to make a good impression on the conservative CMA board, and if that meant a haircut, so be it. This was no time for false pride.

Tommy looked at his father and tried to put on a brave face. His dad smiled back, as if to say, 'You can do it, son.' Many times they had clashed over issues great and small. But today they stood together, and it felt good. Since his arrival, his father had been an enormous help to him and to the others. His sharp legal mind had impressed Charles, Jeff Frazier, and the FBI agents. When Jake Friedman spoke, people listened. Tommy was proud of his father, and he wanted his father to be proud of him.

J.W. Faust exited the boardroom and quickly approached the group. "Okay, they're ready for Tommy."

"May I accompany my son?" Jake asked.

"I mean no disrespect to you, sir, and none to you, Charles, but the board might be intimidated by a couple of lawyers."

Jake and Charles nodded their understanding, only too familiar with the reactions lawyers provoke.

"What does it feel like in there?" Tommy asked J.W.

"It feels... tense. I think their hearts are in the right place, but several members are very skeptical. This is a rather unprecedented thing we're asking."

"Any last minute advice?" Tommy asked as he straightened his tie.

"Just tell the truth. Be firm but don't get emotional. They mainly want to hear from you exactly what Armadas said. Remember, you're the only one who has personal knowledge of the ransom demand. If they don't believe you, we don't have a chance. Well, we better go in. They're waiting for us."

Tommy entered the boardroom and sat down next to Faust. The meeting was chaired by Mrs. Randall, one of the most powerful people in country music. She was an institution on Music Row, and she ran the CMA with a velvet-covered fist. A dignified woman who commanded respect, she spoke first. "Thank you for coming today, Mr. Price. I'm sorry it is under these circumstances."

"Thank you for inviting me, Mrs. Randall. Everyone concerned about Jonetta is very appreciative. I'm also sorry about the circumstances."

"Mr. Price, Agent Faust has painted the big picture for us. But we want to hear it from the horse's mouth. Excuse the expression. I mean we want to hear from you exactly what Hector Armadas said when he made his ransom demand."

"Yes ma'am. Certainly. Hector Armadas personally told me he wanted five minutes on the next CMA awards show.

He said he wanted to address the nation. He didn't say why, and he didn't indicate what he wanted to talk about. But he was very emphatic. He said if he didn't receive the air time, he would execute Jonetta. He used that word, 'execute.' I remember he said he would send her body back to Nashville in a pine box. He also admitted that he had ordered the 'execution' of Sonny Boy McDaniel. I got the clear..."

Tommy was interrupted when a board member stuck his hand in the air and shouted, "Madam chairwoman! Madam chairwoman! I *demand* to be recognized." Tommy realized it was the country music star Model T. Ford. Model T. was well past his prime as an entertainer but he held on to his celebrity with a plowboy's tenacity. His trademark was his red hair. He wore it in an impressive gravity-defying pompadour. His hairdo added four inches to his diminutive, rail thin frame. He reminded Tommy of a bantam rooster. Despite his comic appearance, Ford was also the multimillionaire owner of radio stations, real estate, and race horses. He was a generous patron of right-wing causes and a power within the Republican National Party. Model T. Ford was accustomed to exercising influence and getting his way.

"Madam chairwoman! Please!"

"All right, Chester. You're hereby recognized," Irene said with resignation.

"Thank you. Ladies and gentlemen, I just want to say that never in all my forty some odd years in country music, including over ten years of service as a member of this distinguished board, never have I encountered a more outrageous, outlandish, out and out insane proposition as this fantasy. I flew in last night all the way from Phoenix for this so-called 'emergency' meeting, and I resent this unnecessary waste of my valuable time. The fact that we're even considering going along with this harebrained scheme is enough to make me resign the board in protest. I've always had the highest respect for the FBI. Hell, I *knew* J. Edgar Hoover. Played the ponies with him! But after this morning's presentation, I'm inclined to believe the Bureau's getting soft in the head."

"Chester!" Irene said firmly, as if admonishing an unruly student.

"Irene, don't *Chester* me. I've got a lot more to say, and I won't stop until I've said it." Model T. looked around the room. "People, what are we doing here? Have we lost all common sense? The awards show is our big night. Are we gonna turn it over to some narco-terrorist so he can rant and rave about God knows what and make us the laughing stock of the nation?"

Tommy realized Ford was winning over the group. Heads nodded in agreement. Voices mumbled their approval. He had to do something. He stood up, interrupting the tirade.

"Mr. Ford! Mr. Ford!" Tommy said.

"Son, I believe I still have the floor."

"But Mr. Ford, a girl's life is at stake. Isn't her life worth five minutes of television time?"

Model T. hesitated a moment, then shot back, "Don't be naïve, son. That girl's a goner! Maybe some other fool will give this gangster five minutes of precious national broadcast television. Maybe that bleeding heart, Phil Donahue. But not country music! No sir. Not if I have anything to do with it." Model T. folded his arms over his chest and set his jaw, his face flushed a deep pink.

After an uncomfortable moment of silence, Mrs. Randall spoke quietly but with authority. "Friends, we've got to keep our heads. This is a most difficult situation. I'm torn up, too. But let me say this: I know Jonetta Jordan. I consider her a friend. She's a fine young woman, and she's very popular in this community. This story is hot and getting hotter. I think we could face a major PR disaster if we refuse the FBI and Jonetta comes to harm. I don't want her blood on our hands, staining the good image we've worked so hard to establish. Before we reject the FBI's proposal, I want you all to ponder deeply on the possible repercussions. Mr. Price, why don't you and Agent Faust leave us to our family deliberations. I think we understand the issue before us. Thank you for your assistance."

J.W. and Tommy left the room, realizing that, for better or worse, they had done all they could do. Neither felt very hopeful. Time passed slowly as the board debated Jonetta's fate. After an hour of waiting, Tommy asked Charles to go outside with him. He needed a cigarette, and he had something he wanted to say.

"Charles, this is hard for me to talk about." Tommy felt himself choking up. "But it's because of me that Jonetta got involved in this whole mess. It's my fault. It's my responsibility. I'm so, so sorry." Tommy was fighting back tears.

Charles shook his head. "No, no. That's not right. JJ's a big girl. She knew what she was getting into. We talked about it. I don't blame you, and I'm sure she doesn't either."

"Man, I'm glad you feel that way. But if I had only called someone else instead of her..."

Charles paused and looked straight at Tommy. "I've wondered about that. Why did you call her? Why not the newspaper? Or the police?"

Tommy was ready to confess. "The truth is, I wanted to meet her. I had a crush on her. It was an excuse to get to know her. I... I thought she was cute."

Charles sighed and looked away. "Well, I can't argue with that. I fell pretty hard, too. That's something we have in common. And I bet we're not the only ones."

"Look, Charles, I'm gonna do everything, I mean everything, in my power to get her back. And we will get her back. I just want one thing."

"What's that?"

"An invitation to the wedding."

"You got it." Charles laughed for the first time in days. "You know, you dress up pretty nice for a white boy. I might even make you a groomsman."

"Thanks, Charles. You're a good man."

"And so are you, my friend." They hugged each other, and at that moment, Tommy's romantic feelings for Jonetta ended forever. His long obsession with her lifted, and he regarded her from then on as a very close friend, almost like a sister.

THIRTY FIVE

At 4:30 in the afternoon, as usual, a waiter came to Jonetta's room with iced tea and chocolate cookies. She welcomed his arrival, since it broke the monotony of her long days. Lucinda added sweetener to their drinks and served Jonetta, as the waiter excused himself.

"Cheers, señorita," Lucinda said, raising her glass.

"Cheers, Lucinda."

Within a few moments of sipping her tea, Jonetta sensed a change in her perceptions. She felt like she was falling down a tunnel, and her head was spinning wildly. Across the room, Lucinda had fallen asleep in her chair. Jonetta's mind was swirling and dancing, and she felt profoundly sleepy. She fought unconsciousness, but lost the struggle and fell back in bed, melting into oblivion.

Fifteen minutes earlier in the kitchen, Ed Green had spiked their drinks with a useful Colombian drug called *burundanga*, a white, tasteless powder which causes extreme incapacitation and renders its victims defenseless. An overdose could induce coma or death. He followed the waiter to their room, undetected.

Green had a key to every lock on La Ponderosa, including the one on Jonetta's door. As he entered, he saw that both women were deeply sedated. Lucinda was tempting. She had slid down in the chair, and her dress was hiked around her waist. Her legs were open and he could see her sheer panties and her dark, bulging patch. Indeed, very tempting. He became excited. He had been attracted to Lucinda for a long time, but she belonged to Francisco, a fearless and valued *sicario* who was extremely jealous about his woman. If he forced himself on Lucinda, he might have to kill Francisco. Otherwise, Francisco might kill him. Anyway, Green knew what he had come for and he would not be deterred. He had been planning this experience for days. He wanted the American black beauty.

From a leather bag resembling a doctor's satchel he removed four pieces of nylon rope. He arranged Jonetta spreadeagle on the bed, tying her hands and bare feet to the bedposts. She was wearing a purple tee shirt and blue jeans. Once the ropes were fastened, he took a gleaming scalpel from the bag. He cut her cotton shirt at the neck and ripped it in half, revealing a simple white bra. He put the tip of the scalpel under the bra between the cups and pulled up, moving it back and forth until the bra snapped. Her chest was now exposed. As Green had expected, her breasts were perfect, small and firm. In the cool air her nipples hardened involuntarily. He fondled each breast roughly and bit her nipples. Jonetta stirred and moaned. He glanced at Lucinda to check her condition. She was out cold, having slipped further down in the chair. Her slack, alluring pose taunted him. Perhaps when he finished with Jonetta, he would chance it. After all, he calculated, the *burundanga* should produce an amnesic effect. The women might not remember enough to implicate him.

He returned his attention to Jonetta, studying her jeans. He took a small pair of sharp scissors from the bag, then cut each leg of her jeans along the inseam, from her feet to her crotch. He cut through her beltline and carefully pulled back the splayed denim from her skin. She was wearing white bikini briefs. He picked up the scalpel and pressed it flat against her pubis, probing.

Then he ran the razor sharp blade down her thigh, pressing hard enough to draw blood, but Jonetta did not react. He traced the cut with his fingertip and tasted her blood. As he placed the scalpel under the elastic waistband of her panties, a muscular arm covered with bristling blonde hair encircled his neck and jerked him back. He dropped the knife. Then he felt a strong, sweaty forearm press against the side of his face, placing his head in a powerful human vise. When it broke, his neck popped loudly. The second cervical vertebra dislocated and ripped his spinal cord. He fell to the floor, limp except for his last erection. Before leaving the room, Ed Green's killer untied the ropes restraining Jonetta and tenderly covered her nakedness with a blanket.

THIRTY SIX

In a close vote, the CMA denied the FBI's request, citing a desire to "stand up to terrorism." As Irene had warned, the decision served only to fan the flames of the public's interest in Jonetta and her plight. Her face appeared on the covers of *Time, Newsweek, People,* and countless tabloids. On *Larry King Live* Jesse Jackson raised the specter of race, asking, "If Jonetta Jordan were white, would the Country Music Association come to her rescue?" Other television shows offered air time to Armadas, but he was adamant and specific in his demand. The CMA awards show would be his forum, or else.

A week before the deadline, Charles negotiated an appearance for himself, Tommy, and Ethel on Oprah Winfrey's talk show. Accompanied by agents Tilden and Faust, the group flew to Chicago to promote the cause at what promised to be a sympathetic venue. Despite bad knees and a bout of high blood pressure, Ethel insisted on participating in the trip. "I'm her mother. If I'm on the show, we'll get better ratings," she shrewdly observed. No one could argue with her logic.

Before the show, Oprah attempted to put each of them at ease. She was especially sensitive to Ethel, holding her hand and praying with her. Charles and Oprah had become acquainted two years before when he had directed an endowment drive for their alma mater, Tennessee State University. With Oprah serving as honorary chairwoman of the drive, Charles had raised over ten million desperately needed dollars for TSU, the state's premier black university.

The success of the campaign had made him a hero in Nashville's black community. But as he told Oprah with a shaky voice, "I'd give every dollar we raised to bring her back. That and more. I'd give my own life to save hers."

Tommy observed these black people caring for each other and he envied them. When Oprah approached him with a word of encouragement, he asked her, "Would you introduce me as Price Friedman?"

"Price Friedman? Tommy, this is hardly the time for a name change."

"I know it sounds crazy, but Price Friedman is my real name. I want to use it today. It's important to me. Please."

Oprah studied the young man and read the determination in his eyes. "Okay. But don't be surprised if I call you Tommy by mistake."

"Thank you," he said.

Oprah was true to her word, introducing him to twenty million people as Price Friedman. But, she didn't stop there.

"Price, everyone back in Nashville knows you as Tommy Price. But today, before we went on the air, you asked me to call you by your real name, Price Friedman. Can you tell us why? I'm curious."

"Yes, Oprah, you're right. A lot of people know me as Tommy Price. But that's my stage name. Until recently, I had ambitions to be an entertainer. But I'm not *really* Tommy Price. I'm Price Friedman. A lot of other people watching today know me by that name. In my own small way, I'm trying to be more honest." The studio audience applauded warmly and Oprah smiled. Tommy knew his dad was watching in Passaic and he hoped he was smiling, too. Slowly, Thomas Price Friedman was finding himself.

Using all his skill as an advocate, Charles argued Jonetta's case before a jury of millions. He asked the viewers to protest the CMA's decision. He held up a hand printed sign with the CMA's address, telephone and fax numbers.

Price made the point that a person's life was certainly worth five minutes of television time. Oprah confirmed she had offered Armadas thirty minutes on her show, but he had declined.

A young woman in the audience asked Price, "Do you feel responsible for getting Jonetta mixed up in this thing?"

The question stung like a slap across the face. But, Price responded in a steady voice, "Yes, in many ways, I do blame myself. And I only wish I could trade places with her."

Charles quickly interjected, "Tommy, I mean Price, shouldn't be held responsible. He had information he wanted to share with someone in the media. For whatever reason, he chose to contact Jonetta. Like a good journalist she pursued the story. Price has worked night and day on Jonetta's behalf. We're all in this together."

The audience appreciated Charles' show of solidarity. Then Oprah asked Ethel if she would like to have the final word. Ethel gathered her thoughts and then spoke slowly, "Oprah, I'd like to ask all the prayer groups out there to include Jonetta in their prayers. I believe in the power of prayer, and I believe in miracles. We need a miracle to bring her home. And please, don't pray only for my baby. Pray for the man who took her and the one who makes that evil drug. Pray for them to send Jonetta home. No one is beyond God's mighty love, not even those who do the devil's work."

After their well-received appearance on Oprah's show, the crusade to save Jonetta gathered powerful momentum. But despite a flood of calls, letters, and faxes, the CMA would not reconsider its refusal to meet Hector's ransom. Time was slipping away.

THIRTY SEVEN

In Hector's study Mason faced his angry associate. Hector was seated at his desk and behind him stood Carlos, who stared at Mason with undisguised contempt. Mason realized he was in mortal danger. Perhaps his reservoir of good fortune was exhausted, depleted by a lifetime of risktaking. Armadas had always been the one he couldn't outsmart or manipulate. Bringing a hostage to La Ponderosa had strained his relationship with Hector to the breaking point. Now, *this*. His bodyguard was the primary suspect in Ed Green's murder. He wiped the sweat from his upper lip and swallowed hard, waiting for Armadas to speak.

"The American was very valuable to me. In fact, he was indispensable. That crazy bastard would do anything. He was a monster, but he was *my* monster. Now the *sicarios* have no leader. They demand revenge, and so do I," Hector said coldly.

"But you're their leader, Don Hector. It's you they follow," Mason replied.

"I'm only their employer. Green was one of them, and in their own way, they loved him. As we speak, drunken *sicarios* are roaming my estate, and they're a little *loco*. What do I tell them? How do I satisfy their demands?" Mason didn't answer. He waited for Hector to continue. "A maid saw your bodyguard running from the girl's room about the time of the murder. What was he doing there?"

"I don't know, Don Hector. I was with you. Remember? We were playing golf."

Hector motioned to Carlos. "Bring the fat man in for interrogation." Carlos left the room and returned with Bobby, who was pale and frightened. His hands were tied and his shirt was soaked with perspiration. Two *sicarios* carrying submachine guns accompanied him. They marched him before Armadas, then forced him to get down on his knees.

"Did you kill Colonel Green?" Hector spoke with controlled rage. Bobby turned to Mason, his eyes pleading for assistance. "Look at me when I speak to you! Answer my question. DID YOU KILL COLONEL GREEN?" Hector shouted.

Paralyzed by fear, Bobby stammered, "Uh, uh, uh, uh..."

"If you don't answer my question, I'll have your tongue cut out." As if on cue, one of the *sicarios* produced a knife and held it under Bobby's nose. This only frightened him more and rendered him completely speechless.

"Don Hector, may I talk to him?" Mason asked politely. Hector nodded. Mason spoke soothingly, "Bobby, don't be afraid. Just tell the truth. Did you know Ed Green?"

"Is he the one with the shaved head? The American?"

"Yes, that's him."

"Yeah, I knew him," Bobby said softly.

"Did you hurt him?"

"No, Boss. I swear. It wasn't me."

"But somebody said they saw you leaving the girl's room, about the time he was murdered. Is that wrong?"

"No."

"No, what? Were you in the room?"

"Yes. But..."

"But what, Bobby? What were you doing there?"

"Boss, you told me to guard the girl. You said, be sure she don't get hurt. I saw the door was open. I went in and the bald headed guy was on the floor. He was already dead. The girl was asleep. I got scared and I ran."

"Why didn't you come get me?"

"I tried but I couldn't find you. I swear I didn't do it."

Hector stood up, satisfied he had heard enough. "Take him away and lock him up! I'll deal with him later." After Bobby had been removed, Hector circled Mason like a predator.

"An innocent man doesn't run," Hector said to no one in particular.

"He denied he did it, Don Hector," Mason offered.

"Of course, he denied it. Wouldn't you?"

"Well, yes. But in my country, you're innocent until proven..."

"We're not in your country!" Hector thundered. "We're in *my* country. And within the boundaries of La Ponderosa, I am the law. And I say, an INNOCENT MAN DOESN'T RUN!"

Mason had never seen Hector so enraged. Never mind Bobby, Mason was now afraid for himself. As if Hector had read his fears, he began another line of reasoning.

"I believe a master should be responsible for the actions of his servants. Do you agree, Señor Reed?"

"Not necessarily, Don Hector. It all depends," Mason said nervously.

"On what does it depend?"

"Circumstances. If a servant disobeys the master, the master shouldn't be held responsible. The servant should be punished, not the master. I told Bobby to be on his best behavior while we were here. I specifically told him not to hurt anyone."

"But you also told him to protect the girl. Didn't you?"

"Yes, I did. But not to hurt anyone. He should have contacted one of your staff, but, you see, he's practically retarded. He didn't handle the situation as he should have. He should pay for his mistake. I leave it up to you to decide his punishment. In this situation you are the master."

Hector returned to his chair. He looked out the window, thought for a moment and then chuckled. "Mason, you would make a good lawyer. You're very persuasive."

Mason sighed and smiled at his formidable partner. "Thank you, Don Hector."

Hector waved his hand. "You misunderstood me. I didn't mean it as a compliment. I hate lawyers. But you would make a good one."

Thirty Eight

Over a thousand marchers assembled at the southern end of Sixteenth Avenue in front of Belmont University, approximately one mile from the CMA headquarters. They were peaceful, almost serene. An autumn chill permeated the evening air, reminding Price of football weather. He studied the crowd, amazed at its size and diversity. Black and white, old and young mingled together, many holding the candles volunteers had passed out. Others carried torches, which blazed dramatically above the flickering candles. The effect of carried fire was direct, primal. In a few moments, Price Friedman would climb makeshift steps to a crude platform and speak to these people. He felt exuberant but lightheaded. He hadn't eaten solid food in three days, since the Oprah show, when he had announced he would fast to protest the CMA's position.

David Kraselsky, his former assistant, approached him. "Man, I can't believe how many people showed up," David said. "And all the media, too. Half the kids from TSU are out here, and hundreds from Belmont. Are you nervous?"

"A little. Thanks for getting the sound system. I really appreciate all your help."

"Glad to do it. It's a noble cause." David glanced at his wristwatch. "Hey, it's showtime. We're on a tight schedule."

"Yep. It's time. Well, here goes nothing." Price climbed the wobbly steps and took his position on the stage. He checked the microphone and a blast of feedback startled him. He stepped back from the mic and began. "Friends, may I have your attention? Can you hear me in the back?"

"Yes, fine," someone shouted.

"Good evening, everyone. Thank you for coming out to show your support for our friend in need, Jonetta Jordan." The crowd applauded. "Tonight is a solemn occasion. The business we are about is serious. A person's life is at stake. A very special person." He paused to subdue his emotions. "As I said, this is a serious occasion. Please keep that in mind as we proceed down Sixteenth Avenue to the CMA headquarters. The city has given us one hour for our march and demonstration. After that, I'm asking you to disband quickly and leave the Music Row area peacefully. Please stay in the street and do not, I repeat, *do not* walk on or disturb any private property. Be very careful with those candles and torches, and please don't litter, either. We want to make a good impression. Remember, the whole world is watching!"

The crowd responded with shouts and whistles. Price continued, "When we get to the CMA offices Jonetta's mother, Mrs. Ethel Jordan, will present our petition, containing over seven thousand names, to a CMA representative. Now, before we begin our march, I'd like to ask the Reverend Jerome Grant, who has been Jonetta's personal minister for more than twenty years, to lead us in a word of prayer."

Price extended a hand to Reverend Grant, a large, elderly man with white hair and dark brown skin. He mounted the stage with some difficulty, but when he began to speak, he was in total command.

"Brothers and sisters, please bow your heads. Lord God, all knowing and all mighty, we come to you tonight with fervent hearts. Help us in our efforts to help your precious child, sister Jonetta Jordan. Guide us as we seek to persuade those with earthly powers to join our crusade. Father, we believe our cause is just, right, and good. If we err in pursuit of our purposes, please forgive us, dear Lord. Our mistakes are well-intentioned. We pray that you enter the hearts and minds of your wayward children in South America who have imprisoned our beloved Jonetta. Show them the evil of their ways and return them to the path of righteousness. We also pray that you aid us in our effort to convince the good people at the Country Music Association to reverse their position and to stand with us, united. We ask that you grant them generosity of spirit, and the courage to do the right thing. Finally, dear God, we ask that you send your angels to protect and comfort Jonetta in her time of need. Surround her with your loving grace; pour out your spirit upon her soul; give her the strength to survive her terrible ordeal. We ask these blessings in the holy name of our savior, Jesus Christ. Amen."

The candlelight parade was led by Price, Rev. Grant, Gus, Susan, Ruby, and Mavis. Charles pushed Ethel in a wheelchair and she carried the heavy petition in her lap. Behind them walked Jonetta's numerous friends and associates and hundreds of her well wishers and supporters. Those who weren't holding candles or torches carried signs. SAVE JONETTA. DO THE RIGHT THING. FIVE MINUTES = ONE LIFE. They chanted:

> *Hey, hey, CMA,*
> *It's up to you to save JJ!*
> *Hey, hey, CMA,*
> *It's up to you to save JJ!*

And:

> *One, two*
> *Three, four, five!*
> *Bring Jonetta home alive!*

In her den on Belle Meade Boulevard, Irene Randall sipped a potent scotch and water and studied the events, live on Channel Six. As the crowd gathered outside the CMA building, she shook her head in dismay and muttered to herself, "What a mess. What a godawful mess."

Then she picked up the telephone and placed a call to Phoenix, Arizona. She was thinking about firing Chester Ford's longtime girlfriend, Betty Sue, a CMA receptionist whose main function was to keep Model T.'s motor running on his frequent trips to Nashville. Irene liked Betty Sue. But, she also liked Chester's long suffering wife, Marilyn. And Betty Sue kept making dumb little mistakes, all of which Irene had carefully documented for the record, just in case. No, she *really* didn't want to fire Betty Sue and cause Chester any trouble. But, if she had to, she would.

"Hello, Chester. Irene. Listen..."

THIRTY NINE

Partly to appease the *sicarios* and partly to satisfy his own penchant for pomp and circumstance, Hector staged an elaborate memorial service for Green at the polo field. Hector wanted a good turnout, so he required all the residents of La Ponderosa to attend, excepting only the plantation's children and their attendants. Jonetta was there, still groggy and disoriented three days after Green's attack. Mercifully, the *burundanga* had prevented almost all memory of her ordeal. The painful wound on her inner thigh and the scrapes on her wrists and ankles were disturbing mysteries to her, as were her missing clothes. But, she had little desire to understand anything more about the cause of her injuries or the whereabouts of her tee shirt and jeans. She did know that Green had assaulted her and, in turn, had been killed by someone defending her. Lucinda said Bobby was rumored to have murdered Green. Bobby. The idiot who had kidnapped her may have saved her. As she waited for the ceremony to begin, she contemplated the irony that Bobby represented.

Around the perimeter of the field American and Colombian flags flew at half-mast. A brass urn containing Green's ashes was displayed atop a five foot marble pedestal, and behind the urn, a hastily executed oil portrait of the deceased rested on a tripod. On the field, the *sicarios* stood in formation wearing red berets, white gloves, khaki uniforms, and spit polished combat boots. Everyone rose when *Los Banda de La Ponderosa* segued from "The Green, Green Grass of Home" into the Colombian national anthem. Then the musicians managed a ragged but earnest version of "The Star Spangled Banner." Despite his status as a fugitive from American justice, Green had been a loud patriot.

Hector delivered the eulogy, demonstrating an authentic talent for public speaking. Jonetta comprehended practically nothing of his impassioned forty-five minute oration in Spanish. She caught a few words: Indiana, California, Vietnam, Ferdinand Marcos, Idi Amin. At one point Hector held up an old copy of *Soldier of Fortune* magazine with Green on the cover.

Hector concluded his address with a short prayer. Then he left the podium and strode past the *sicarios* to the center of the polo field where he stood motionless, waiting. Within a few minutes a large helicopter appeared from behind a hill, flew to where Hector stood, and then ascended straight up to a great height, at least two thousand feet above the ground. At that point Francisco shouted a command and the *sicarios* executed a snappy about face. All eyes were on Hector as he took a long red scarf from his pocket and waved it over his head. Everyone stood, responding instinctively to the strange drama of the moment.

High above, a man with a black bag over his head appeared in the open doorway of the helicopter. Suddenly, someone pushed him and he dove head first from the chopper. As he fell, he began to tumble head over heels. His arms were tied behind him, but his legs pumped the air like he was riding an invisible bicycle. He tumbled over and over as if in slow motion until he hit the ground with a gruesome thud only twenty yards away from Hector. The fallen body lay very still. Hector walked slowly to the corpse and pushed it over with his foot. He put the scarf on the ground and took a switchblade from his back pocket, then cut the knot securing the black bag and removed it. Bobby's dead eyes were open.

Blood flowed from his mouth where he had bitten his tongue in half. Hector gently closed Bobby's eyes and then cut off the left ear, which he wrapped in the red scarf. He walked back to Francisco and presented the bloody scarf to him. Francisco raised it above his head and shouted "¡VEN-GANZA!,"... revenge. The *sicarios* shouted and shot their pistols in the air, and as the acrid smoke from their weapons drifted around her, Jonetta realized (if she had ever doubted it) that Armadas was capable of anything.

In the row of seats behind her, Gunther Beck looked down at his riding boots. He felt no remorse whatsoever about killing Green. In Gunther's opinion, the former corporal who called himself colonel had long deserved to die. The world was a better place without the cruel American. Indeed, Green was about to do unspeakable things to the girl, whom Gunther also fancied. But the unlucky one-eared wretch lying on the polo field was another matter. It's too bad an innocent man was sacrificed to placate the blood thirsty *sicarios*. But, better him than me, Gunther reasoned. Better him than me.

FORTY

The day before the CMA awards show Irene Randall announced at a hastily convened news conference that Armadas would be given his five minutes. Technical preparations for a satellite feed from Colombia were complete and the CMA was in communication with Hector and his people. She said he had promised her personally that Jonetta would be released safely within twenty-four hours of the show. She declined to specify when during the two hour telecast he was scheduled to appear. When pressed on the issue, she suggested coyly, "Why don't you tune in and find out?"

At La Ponderosa Hector had converted the grand dining room into a makeshift television studio. As he rushed around, shouting orders to technicians and engineers, Elena remarked to her mother that she had never seen him so agitated and nervous.

"What will he talk about, Elena?" her mother asked. Her tone suggested she was afraid he might embarrass the family.

"Mother, I don't know. He's being very secretive about the whole affair. I'm not sure he knows what he will say. But I'm sure he'll think of something."

"Elena, I worry he's getting a little crazy." Elena's mother rolled her eyes.

"He's always been crazy... like a fox." Elena smiled slightly, pleased that her husband had captured the world's attention. He had always amazed her, but she realized this latest gambit would elevate him, at least in the eyes of the

Colombian people, into the realm of myth. It would be his finest moment. She caught his eye and he smiled at her, that smile that always made her heart jump.

At this point, Jonetta had been in Colombia over three weeks, and since the Green incident she had been confined to her room. The strain of her ordeal, the strangeness of her predicament, the acid fear and the numbing isolation were eroding her stability. She hadn't slept well in several days, haunted in part by nightmares of Bobby's grisly demise. Meticulously recording the details of her experience in a journal provided some relief and filled empty hours. Increasingly, she turned to prayer and Elena's Bible. In moments of deep meditation she could feel her mother's presence, always behind her and to the left. Sometimes she sensed her father was also with her. At other times she missed her parents to the point of tears.

Desperate for information, Jonetta bribed Lucinda to perform reconnaissance for her. The pay off? Jonetta's promise of a job in the United States and assistance with immigration. It worked. Within hours of their bargain Lucinda briefed Jonetta on the details of the ransom, having obtained her information from Francisco, the new chief of security. Jonetta could hardly believe the story Lucinda had told her. Hector Armadas on the CMA awards show? It was too fantastic to imagine.

Mason was envious of Hector's coup, and he pressed Armadas to share a mere thirty seconds of air time. Mason had a couple of things he would like to say to Nashville and the world. Hector reluctantly agreed to consider including him if Mason provided a script of his remarks for prior approval. Mason did so and accurately. He knew better than to mislead Armadas. To wit:

Good evening, friends and neighbors. I'm Mason Reed. I wish I could be there with you but circumstances dictate otherwise. Tonight, I have a confession to make. I never did like country music and I never will. I think country music is dumb music for dumb people. Give me Sinatra anytime. Thank you and good night.

Hector angrily rejected Mason's participation. Reed's proposed comments deeply offended Armadas, who truly loved country music. Mason recanted and assured him that he had been joking, but Hector knew better, and he decided, then and there, to terminate his relationship with Reed once conditions normalized. Mason, he realized, lacked *discretion*.

In Nashville, tension levels were rising as showtime approached. The technical problems posed by a feed from La Ponderosa had been solved easily enough, but the CMA's decision was still being debated as the tuxedoed and sequined notables streamed into the Grand Ole Opry House. As to the wisdom of caving in to Armadas, opinions were about evenly divided, but no one disputed that Hector's appearance was eagerly anticipated. It promised to be the most exciting CMA awards show... ever.

Midway through the second hour, right after the presentation for female vocalist of the year, Mrs. Randall walked to the lectern, and a hush fell over the audience. In the twenty-three years she had guided the CMA this was the first time she had appeared on the show. Everyone at the Grand Ole Opry House knew what was coming.

"Good evening, ladies and gentlemen...." The audience rose spontaneously in a booming ovation. Despite her efforts to calm the crowd, the ovation gathered momentum, growing louder and more boisterous.

"Please... please," she motioned them to resume sitting.

But they responded with a roar, punctuated by whistles and foot stomping. Then she realized they were attempting, perhaps unconsciously, to sabotage the whole thing, to prevent it by staging a controlled riot, and that made her mad.

"Damn it, everybody! Sit down and shut up! Let's get this over with so we can go back to business." The shock of hearing the *grande dame's* angry swearing on national television stopped them cold and order was restored. Irene installed a dainty pair of reading glasses at the end of her nose and read from a prepared text. "Recently, as you all know, the board of directors of the Country Music Association voted to provide Mr. Hector Armadas with five minutes of airtime on tonight's show in return for the safe release of his hostage, our friend, Jonetta Jordan. By doing so, the CMA neither endorses nor condones anything Mr. Armadas may say or do tonight. Nor do we endorse nor condone any of Mr. Armadas' activities, especially his role in the international cocaine trade.

"By agreeing to meet Mr. Armadas' demands we are attempting to save someone's life. And now, I want to speak directly to you, Hector Armadas." Irene removed her glasses and looked at the camera. "The world is now a witness to our bargain. Don't disgrace yourself and your country by failing to live up to our agreement. For heaven's sake, free Jonetta Jordan! And now I present live from Medillin, Colombia . . . Hector Armadas."

As Irene left the stage a large screen descended. The houselights went down and the audience became very quiet. The anticipation was palpable. After a slight, unnerving delay, electronic impulses began to flicker and dance on the screen. Then, a clear image emerged. It was Hector sitting on a stool, one foot on the floor, dressed informally, smiling.

"*Buenas noches.* My name is Hector Armadas Galéna. I

am very happy to be with you tonight, and I appreciate this opportunity to visit with you. There are many things I would like to say, but my time is limited, so I must hurry. First of all, I want to say how much I love country music. Country music is truly the music of America. I love so many things about the United States. That is why it makes me so sad that your government, in effect, has declared war on me. Because of this unfortunate state of affairs, I cannot come to America and enjoy firsthand the attractions you take for granted, like the Grand Ole Opry, a place I have always wanted to visit.

"Amigos, this war on drugs is crazy. I am a businessman, I'm not a warrior! To be successful in business you must find a need and fill it. That is what I do. Nothing more, nothing less. Many people enjoy our product. Perhaps some of you have tried our product and like it. It is not for everybody, and personally, I don't use it. But I will fight for your right to do so. Isn't that what America is all about? Personal freedom? I do believe some type of drug legalization accompanied by governmental regulation would be better for America. And if someone abuses cocaine and develops a dependency, they should receive medical treatment, not a jail sentence!

"But, I'm not here tonight to talk about drugs or politics. I'm here because of music." Hector paused, looked to his left, and Carlos appeared, holding a Spanish guitar. Carlos smiled sheepishly and handed the guitar to his brother. Hector continued, "*Gracias*, Carlos. Many years ago I began to write songs. So far, I have written over one hundred songs, mostly in Spanish but some in English. For several years I have been sending my songs to publishers and record companies in Nashville, the songwriting capital of the world. But, to my disappointment, the envelopes are always returned, unopened, stamped: UNSOLICITED MATERIAL NOT ACCEPTED.

"It took me awhile, but I finally have your attention. So, tonight, I will sing a song I wrote. My niece, Esmeralda, will sing harmony. My song is titled, 'The Cowboy Blues.' I hope you like it."

And then Hector sang his song. His tenor voice quavered with a sweet vibrato, but he was in tune. He played simple chords on the guitar as Esmeralda provided a close, tight high harmony. In a room at the Opryland Hotel, Price, Gus, and Susan watched in amazement as Hector Armadas, one of the world's most dangerous and hated men, bared his soul.

When a cowboy sings the blues
There's a teardrop in his song
Like a lonesome whippoorwill
He can sing it all night long
Like a coyot' in the hills
Howling at the yellow moon
He can make the night stand still
With his sad and mournful tune

The cowboy blu -ooh -ooh -oohs is for broken hearts
For the soul who chooses to live apart
No children at his knee
No woman waits at home
A cowboy sings the blues all alone
A cowboy sings the blues all alone

Yodel lay hee
Yodel lay hee
Yodel lay hee hooooooooooooooo

Gus and Price exchanged disbelieving looks, shaking their heads at the incredible moment they had just witnessed.

"He went to all this trouble just to pitch a song!" Price said. "Amazing!"

"He's one of us! A songwriter! Damnedest thing I ever saw," Gus added.

"Not a bad song either," Susan said.

"Not bad at all," Price said.

"And he was right on the note," Gus said. "Right on it."

Price stood up. "Now we'll see if he's a man of his word."

FORTY ONE

Blindfolded and gagged, her ankles in chains and her wrists bound behind her, Jonetta was led by three *sicarios* to a Ford delivery van. They forced her to lie face down and one of the men placed his heavy boot between her shoulderblades. She could hardly breathe, but she didn't dare complain.

She was terrified. She knew that within a short time she would either be released or murdered. It was that simple. Her hopes for survival were strengthened by the words Elena had said as they bid farewell that morning.

"Jonetta, I hope God blesses you with many children and a long life to enjoy them. Please tell the people in your country that the Colombians are a good people caught in bad circumstances." Then Elena had given her a tight hug.

But Jonetta knew her fate was in the hands of the *sicarios*, not Elena. Because of Jonetta, they had lost their beloved leader, Colonel Green. Perhaps their bloodlust for revenge had not been satisfied by Bobby's sacrifice. She prayed continuously as the van bumped over rough, unpaved country roads. She detected the sweet smells of the countryside. At least if I die, she thought, it will be among the trees and flowers, observed by the birds and hidden fauna. Somehow that thought soothed her.

The men with her said very little to each other and nothing to her. Though it was early in the morning, their bodies gave off strong odors as if they had been working all day in the field. She prayed especially that she would not be raped. Please God.

Suddenly, the van came to jolting halt, throwing her head against the bottom of a metal seat. She saw stars behind her closed eyes. Her fear increased.

Two men roughly pulled her from the vehicle feet first. She fell hard on the ground, but it was covered with a soft cushion of grass, and she wasn't injured.

Then the men turned her over and she lay on her back. They stood around her and talked among themselves. It seemed an eternity as she awaited their next move. Finally, she felt hands on her legs and she shuddered, preparing herself for the worst.

But the worst never came. Instead, they unlocked her ankle chain. Then, they removed the gag from her mouth. But they did not remove her blindfold nor untie her hands. She heard them getting in the van. The motor started.

Reflexively, she called out. "Wait! What can I do?" Instantly, she regretted having said anything.

She heard them laughing. One of them shouted as they sped away, "Scream!"

For hours Jonetta stood there and screamed. She would count to one hundred and then shout, "Help!" Over and over, as the sun climbed its arc, as the insects buzzed around her, she cried for help.

A little before noon, three hours into her ordeal, a dog found her, sniffing her feet, barking at the odd sight he had discovered. She spoke to the dog like it was human. "Go get help. Be a good dog and go get somebody." The dog left and then she felt lonely. She could have walked but she was afraid to, fearing she might fall or stumble or run into something.

She had nothing with her, no provisions, no money and she realized if she wasn't discovered fairly quickly, she might die from exposure or wild animals.

So she counted to one hundred and screamed.

She heard voices! Not one or two but a whole group talking excitedly, coming closer. They surrounded her. She was in the middle of a circle of people, but their voices sounded strange, high pitched and sing-songy. She felt little hands on her and she drew back. Something about the size of a large monkey jumped on her back! She screamed again from the startle. Then she felt her blindfold being undone. It fell from her eyes. The sun blinded her and she tried to make out the figures around her. As her eyes adjusted to the light, she realized she was surrounded by . . . children! A dozen or more beautiful children. The oldest, a lovely girl of fourteen or so, took Jonetta's hand and said, "Come. Go home. Come. Go home."

Tears were streaming down her face as Jonetta nodded her head and replied,

"Sí! Sí! Home! Home!"

THE END

EPILOGUE

Jonetta returned home safely. In short order, she married Charles and they moved to Atlanta, where she works as a reporter for CNN. Her account of her ordeal, *Hostage!*, spent thirty-seven weeks on *The New York Times* non-fiction best seller list. Film rights are being negotiated. With the advance money from her book, Charles and Jonetta bought a Tudor mansion in one of Atlanta's toniest neighborhoods, complete with a guest house where Ethel lives. Despite Jonetta's objections, Ethel insisted on bringing the red La-Z-Boy. Charles joined a prominent law firm and is contemplating a run for the city commission. The Robinsons hope to start a family in the near future.

Price left Nashville and enrolled in law school at NYU, his father's alma mater. Although his studies monopolize his time, he keeps his guitar tuned and his notebook handy, in case inspiration strikes. Last month he fell in love with Amy, a fellow law student. She loves him, too.

As of this writing, Gus lives very comfortably in a shrimping village south of Matamoros on the Gulf Coast. His royalties go much further in Mexico, and the climate suits him. He's learning Spanish with the help of his companion, Angelina, a lusty gap-toothed lady half his age. He also keeps his Martin guitar well tuned and close by. On Saturday nights he plays in a *tejano* band, just for fun.

Susan remained in Nashville and is making a go of her own independent record label, Songbird, which is devoted to "preserving and promoting the work of great American songwriters." After re-establishing relations with her parents, her father provided the seed money to start the label. Gus was her first signing, but he's taking his time choosing the songs he wants to record, which drives Susan to distraction.

Ruby and Mavis moved to Branson, Missouri, and opened "Ruby McDaniel's World Famous Good Time Song and Dance Theater." Business has exceeded their wildest expectations. The highlight of Ruby's show is an emotional tribute to her late son, "The Sun Shines in My Sonny Boy's Eyes." She also does a nice job on "Wayward Angel."

Having fallen out of favor with Hector, Mason left Colombia shortly after the telecast. He lives a demanding existence, constantly traveling, utilizing aliases and disguises to elude the pursuing authorities. He retained an attorney in Miami to plea bargain on his behalf. He wants to return to the United States and pay his debt to society, preferably in a four-star federal prison.

Six weeks after his appearance on the CMA awards show, Hector was gunned down by Colombian state police as he left the Medillin home of his mistress, Consuela Diego, who sold him out for one million dollars. Over thirty thousand mourners attended his funeral, which was broadcast live on Colombian television. Like Sonny Boy, Hector didn't live to enjoy the success of his song, "The Cowboy Blues."

Despite much criticism and controversy, John Farley Stringer's recording of the tune reached *Billboard's* top twenty on the country music chart. It would have gone higher, but Ernie Cox never got on board.

Hector's appearance on the CMA awards show was seen by over one billion people worldwide, the largest audience to see a country music show, before, since, and probably, ever.

ABOUT THE AUTHOR

Dan Tyler was born and raised in Mississippi. After graduating from law school, he moved to Nashville, Tennessee to practice law and write songs. Since then, dozens of his tunes have been recorded by major artists including Kenny Rogers, Eddie Rabbitt, Juice Newton, Dr. Hook, The Nitty Gritty Dirt Band, B.J. Thomas, Keith Whitley, The Oak Ridge Boys, and LeAnn Rimes. Five of his songs have reached the top of the country music charts: "Hearts on Fire," "Bobbie Sue," "Modern Day Romance," "Baby's Got a New Baby," and "Twenty Years Ago."

Dan currently lives in Nashville with his wife, Adele, and their two children, William and Elise. *Music City Confidential* is his first novel.

ACKNOWLEDGMENTS

Writing a book is a solitary affair; publishing one requires a team effort. Many thanks to Richard Courtney and Harold McAlindon at Eggman Publishing and their helpful staff, past and present. A special thanks to Chris Shook at Type-Byte Graphix. Her dedication and attention to detail made this a better book. It is a particular joy that my brother, Bill, designed the cover. Thank you R.S. Field, for the title suggestion. I'd like to thank my many friends and family for their support and encouragement, especially my mother, Margie Fairchild Tyler. She got me started, in more ways than one.